Cruel Black Hearts

Candace Wondrak

Chapter One – Stella

What makes a killer?

I'm not talking about a man's skin and bones, but rather what shaped them—what led them down the dark and bloody path they took. We are the same, universally, technically, but no one can deny there is a stark difference between the good and the evil. The killers and the saviors.

And of course, you know me. This article isn't about crimes of passion, because we're all capable of angry fits of violence, some worse than others. When I say what makes a killer, what I really mean is, what makes a *serial* killer. What makes someone kill multiple people in a premeditated manner on multiple separate occasions, usually in the same gruesome way?

Serial killers have always been fascinating to the public eye, and I myself would freely admit to being one of those people. The newscasts, the court hearings—I'm obsessed just as much as the next American. Like an addict, I can't get enough, which I suppose is why I always submit articles like these for the Wednesday issue of the Local Tribune.

But it doesn't matter much, because here you are, still reading. That means you are just as much a slave to this as I am. It's good for you, really, because I'm going to tell you something the psychologists won't, something the media would never dare to air on their news stations. It is a truth that might rock your imaginative foundation of serial killers, though if you're like me, you'll find it not so surprising.

Here is the truth most don't want to hear: serial killers are just like you and me. They are us, and we are them. You could not pick a serial killer out of a lineup, couldn't sense a serial killer stalking you on the street. They tend to blend, which is what we, as humans, are so good at. Avoiding the public eye, pretending not to be interesting. Serial killers are masters of disguise, masters of their bloody craft. It's why some of their sprees last decades.

Sure, some of them may have had bad childhoods. Some of them may have been abused physically, mentally, sexually. Some of them are outcasts, the weird one in the class as you were growing up. But I bring to you this point—not all bad childhoods shape children into would-be serial killers, and not every quiet, weird kid in your class turned out to be someone like Jeffrey Dahmer or Ed Gein. It is, almost scarily, hard to point and predict who will grow up to become the next BTK.

And if you're somehow able to, head on over to the FBI. I'm sure they'd love to have you.

Psychologists would say there's an imbalance in their brains, that they're missing a key component to human life, to human emotion—empathy. And logically, we all agree because it makes sense. Who could end someone else's life—who could peel skin from bone and make lampshades out of the dried leather? Surely not someone who feels empathy for their victims.

Again, I'm going to play the devil's advocate and say that we, as a society, lack empathy. We shame each other, we blame the victims of violent crime, tell our homeless it's their fault they're living on the streets. We do not take responsibility for anyone else, and I would go so far as to say we don't care about anyone else besides ourselves.

Am I wrong?

Can you prove it?

What makes a killer? Research and the news stations would have you believe it's all figured out, but I'm here to tell you it's not that simple. I'm here to tell you the answer to the question.

We don't know.

The laptop screen was a little too bright for me, so I tapped the brightness button a few times, dimming the screen as I reread what I wrote. I sipped my coffee— black, no sugar, no cream. Its bitter taste was still hot as it fell down my throat.

I sat in the coffee shop I always sat in when I wrote my articles for the Local Tribune. A small-town store with only a dozen tables and old machines that were loud and rusted. The new Starbucks down the street had nearly put them out of business, but there would always be people like me, people who refused to change.

Change was not always a good thing, I knew from past experience.

After saving the document, my eyes checked the time. Shit. I had exactly ten minutes to email the article to my boss and make a run down the street and across traffic to the Tribune's offices. I quickly did what I had to, shut my laptop and finished the last few sips of coffee. As I worked to shove my laptop in my messenger bag, I felt someone's eyes on me.

I looked up, meeting the light green eyes of a man sitting a few tables away. He didn't look much older than me; if anything, he looked a year or two younger. I was only twenty-five, still a baby by today's standards. But hey, at least I wasn't living with my parents anymore; I rented a house in town with my best friend from high school. We weren't too far from our hometown, but far enough we didn't have to worry about seeing anyone we knew from high school while we went out and shopped for groceries. People didn't like me, usually. For whatever reason.

But back to the man.

I wasn't supermodel gorgeous, and my brown hair was just thrown up in a messy bun. I had no cleavage showing, as I wore a simple black T-shirt that came up to my neck and covered my arms. Jeans and boots. A normal outfit for the sometimes warm, sometimes cold weather we had here. My mom always said I was pretty, unique, but I didn't think so. Other than my one defining characteristic, I thought I was average all around.

It was my heterochromia. My left eye was a warm, amber brown, the color of milk chocolate. But my right eye? It was a startlingly bright and luminous blue. When people looked at me, they often commented on my unique stare, how pretty it was.

It was ridiculous and infuriating how much a single blue eye could change people's perspective of you. But then, of course, when they got to know me, I wasn't just some pretty girl with strange eyes. I was strange all around, which worked out well, because I didn't like most people. I was nice and friendly to them, but did I want to hang out with them? Not necessarily. Callie was the only friend I needed.

I locked eyes with the man. He was cute enough, but he didn't call out to me. Short brown hair, a few shades lighter than my own. He seemed rather skinny, but maybe it was because he was sitting.

Once our stares met, it was a wordless battle. Who would look away first?

Me, because I had a meeting to get to.

Scooting out of my seat, I slung my bag over my shoulder and went for the door. I threw out the coffee cup, using my back to push on the glass door. It was…so annoying, having people look at me like I was some circus freak all because my eyes were different. Granted, doctors have said the difference in color was nearly unheard of for anyone with heterochromia, but it was just an excuse to me.

A doctor's excuse for other people to stare at me.

I didn't like being stared at. The inherent intrusive nature of being stared at never sat well with me. Just like the killers in my articles—and the ones in real life, I suppose—I wanted to fly under the radar, have no extra attention on me. It wasn't too much to ask. Let me be just another cog in the machine that was human society.

The sun was bright overhead as I hurried down the sidewalk, jaywalking once no cars were passing by. The homey coffee shop was at the edge of the business district of town, and the Tribune's offices were somehow smack dab in the middle, nestled between the banks and the restaurants and the big department stores.

It was nearly one, which meant I had to take it up a notch, otherwise I'd be late, and then Killian would never let me hear the end of it. He always tried to hold me to higher standards than the others, for whatever reason.

It was annoying.

I hurried along, practically running by the time the Tribune's office building came into view. A small one-story building, nothing impressive at all about it. At one point in time, it used to be another bank, but the bank went out of business. However the hell that worked. But, anyway, the Tribune bought it, did a little construction to make its interior a wide-open space, and boom—the local newspaper was moved from an old, outdated building to an actual business establishment.

It happened like twenty years ago, so I wasn't quite sure of the story, since I was a whopping five years old at the time, but it's what Killian said.

The front doors to the office gave me little resistance as I pushed inside, meeting the messy interior of the building. Desks, desks, and more desks, all with computers and stacks of papers, were arranged in the front area. Filing cabinets lined both sides of the walls, Killian's private office in the back. There was a separate part of the building where the newspaper was printed, but I never went back there. I didn't need to.

I went to my desk, hanging my bag's strap against the back of my chair, pulling out my laptop as a woman walked past me and muttered, "You almost didn't make it." Sandy, I think her name was? A nice enough woman. Middle-aged, recently been through a divorce if the white band of skin on her ring finger was any indication. Ever since taking the ring off, she'd opted for low-cut and tight clothes, along with makeup that even Callie wouldn't have worn back in high school.

"I'm here now," I muttered, following her and the other part-time employees to the conference area in the back. Basically just a large round table with swivel chairs, right in front of the glass walls that encased Killian's office. Not an actual private conference room—that would've been too much.

Everyone went to their chosen seats. I knew most of their names, and they knew me, but they didn't often talk to me. Which was just fine, because like I said, I didn't need friends. Friends were just people who you gave the opportunity of disappointing you. It was the sad truth I'd learned in my life. Callie was more than enough.

Some people worked on tablets, others just notepads. I was the only one on a laptop, one that was a few years old, at that. Didn't have the money to replace it yet, so hopefully it lasted. Right now, most of my money went towards rent and the utility bills. Didn't even have a car. Didn't need one.

As I set my laptop down and lifted the top half, Killian came out of his office. He wore fancy black pants and a dark vest over his button-up shirt, the sleeves rolled up like he was a fancy high roller in Vegas. He was a cute enough man, mostly Irish, if his red hair, light eyes, and the enormous number of freckles on his face meant anything.

"Stella," Killian drawled out my name, saying it slowly, much like he always did, "glad to see you've joined us."

How I hated being called out in front of everyone. Being singled out, plucked from the nameless masses, was the one thing I hated above all else. He knew it, yet he still went ahead and did it every time we had a meeting. It was the one thing I could count on from him, and it made me uneasy each time.

I shifted in my seat, feeling immensely uncomfortable as I muttered, "I'm always here." It was true—I never missed a meeting. I was always here, right on time. Never late, never early. Why would I spend more time here than I had to? I never understood the people who arrived at their jobs fifteen minutes early. It was fifteen whole minutes they could've used to do literally anything else.

Killian was not done with me yet. "And your article for this week's paper?"

"Sent it ten minutes ago." My response must've been amusing, because everyone at the table started to chuckle—and then they immediately tried to hide their amusement. I did my best to ignore them. My life did not revolve around other people or their approval, and that included Killian's.

All Killian did was nod along, keeping the *of course you did* to himself. At this point, he shouldn't be surprised. It's what I did, what I've done since day one of this job, and it was what I would continue to do until I quit or was fired—turn in my articles at the last possible second.

The meeting droned on, and I found myself trying to take notes about what the goal was for the next week's papers—the Local Tribune put out a Wednesday paper and a Sunday paper, so it wasn't like I was ever short on work. But I was only part time, just like everyone else. A way the company got around paying for health insurance.

10

It didn't much matter to me, though. I didn't have insurance. If something happened to me, I just wanted to die. Don't waste time trying to save me, you know? I wasn't important.

I was just…me.

When the meeting was over and everyone was packing up to either leave for the day or go back to their desks, Killian caught me. "Stella, can you hang for a bit? There's something I want to talk to you about." He meandered back into his office, wordlessly asking me to follow him, knowing I had to because he was my boss, even though he wasn't too many years older than me.

I never had a problem with Killian. He was a good enough guy, I supposed, but after last year's Christmas party, when he got so drunk he practically threw himself on me…and then threw up on my shoes, well. It was hard to look at him the same way after that. At the time, he'd just gotten over a really bad breakup, so I left it alone, didn't make a big deal about it. Everyone was entitled to their own mental breakdown every now and then. Life was hard.

No, not just hard. Life was an absolute bitch.

I closed my laptop, grabbing it as I stood. Had to hide the blog post I'd started to write instead of taking notes during the meeting. I was finally getting enough internet traffic on my blog to start making some money off it, and I wasn't about to give it up for a part time job. It was a blog I'd started back in high school, when blogging was actually cool.

Although, I was sure there were people out there who never considered it cool. Callie was among them, but she was supportive all the same. Usually.

As soon as I went into his office, he closed the door and shut the blinds. A little weird, and it would surely get the others talking, because they already thought Killian and I were in some sort of secret relationship, but I didn't say anything. I sat in one of the two leather chairs facing his desk, waiting for him to walk around and sit in his large, expensive chair.

He didn't sit in his chair, though; he leaned between me and his desk, like he was trying to be cool or something. If only he knew his efforts were wasted on me.

"Stella," Killian started, crossing his arms. Arms that were, I noticed, a bit more muscled than I thought they were. He was stronger than he first appeared. "I know I gave you permission to write what you wanted to write, but…"

Ah, so this was where he tried to get me to write about other things. Things besides serial killers and the banes of human society. I immediately tuned him out, because nothing else interested me. If he wanted to try and force me to write about the new playground at the local park or the construction zones, he had another thing coming. I'd walk out that damn door and not look back, even though I enjoyed this job. Life was too short to be miserable.

Who the hell knew how long he went on, but he eventually stopped and asked, "Are you even listening to me?"

What could I do? Lie? I wasn't a liar.

"No," I said, holding my head up high, even though I was in the inferior position on the chair.

"I know your…articles have gained a bit of a cult following—they are our most visited articles online, but…" Killian seemed to have difficulties talking.

I wasn't sure what he was trying to say. "Are you firing me?" It was the last thing I needed, but I'd be able to find a job somewhere else fast, especially if the boss was a man. Men always fell for my eyes the hardest, always had the most trouble seeing past them. I was not above using my one defining feature to my advantage when I needed to. I hated to do it, but I would.

"No, no," he quickly said, reaching an arm out to me. He didn't touch me though, because that would've been inappropriate. I was pretty sure he was afraid to try to touch me again, after how he'd acted at the Christmas party. "No, I'm not firing you. I'm just…I'm asking you to try to find something else to write about. At least for the printed paper. You can keep writing your killer articles for our site, but our print subscribers are mostly elderly. I don't think they want to read about serial killers twice a week."

I was slow to nod. I supposed I could try to think of something else to write about, but I would not promise him anything. There was hardly anything else that kept my interest, and if I wasn't interested in what I was writing about, my articles would be shit. The words just didn't flow when my fingers hovered over the keyboard.

"All right. That's all I'm asking." Killian sighed, his eyes dropping below mine. I didn't care where his eyes were, just that our meeting was done.

I said nothing else as I stood and went for the door.

Killian had something more to say, for he was behind me suddenly, grabbing the door before I could. "You know…it's my birthday tomorrow."

Freezing, I wasn't sure what I should do with this information.

"I know you have off, but…the others and I are going out for drinks. You should join us." There was a pause, a bit too long of one, before he yanked the door open and let me escape.

As I hurried away, I knew drinks were the last thing I wanted, especially where Killian was concerned.

Chapter Two - Lincoln

The feeling of hot water on my skin was one of the best feelings in the world. It was right up there with fucking, hunting, and killing. Pure ecstasy. Almost like the water could really get me clean, purify the darkness in my soul.

Did I even have a soul? I guessed it didn't matter much, because if I did, I definitely wasn't going to heaven anytime soon. The bastard upstairs wouldn't even look at me after what I'd done. What I still planned on doing, until the day I got caught.

Because all killers got caught, one way or another. The police, the FBI, or even old age. Sooner or later something would catch up with me, and I wouldn't be able to escape. Not a pleasant thought. I should be thinking of happy thoughts, here in the shower.

Yes, happy thoughts, like our last kill.

I would be the world's biggest liar if I said I didn't get a thrill out of hearing the screams, the chains rattling as our latest prey of the night had tried to escape from our basement of horrors. It was funny in a way, because she'd been more than willing to get tied up on our bed, to be shared between me and Ed. Women were always the easier ones to finagle into coming with us. Men...the men were harder. Some took more convincing than others.

Ed and I had a system. It worked. For years it had worked. We were like brothers, him and I, only not really, because then things would've been weird. But we were alike in all the ways that counted. We got pleasure from the same thing: inflicting pain onto others.

I remembered watching Ed pound into her. He always wore a manic look on his face when his dick was in someone, a smirk he never wore when he wasn't wet from cunt. Then, of course, my mind went to what had happened after. After we'd had our fill of the pretty blonde, after we'd choked her and brought her to the basement.

She'd been a bad girl, and someone didn't want her coming home.

Ed and I never knew the details. We just…did what we had to. In the beginning, at least, I'd get the contact information, and we'd plan the kill, decide whether to stage an accident or bring them home and have some fun first. We weren't assassins in the generic way, and it wasn't so much a family business as it was family courtesy, because my family knew all about my urges, and Ed's, too.

Even without the tips to who had a need for a knife against the throat, Ed and I would still find someone to sate our needs. One way or another, we would kill. We couldn't do without it.

I killed my first when I was young. It was before my family had brought me into the business. It was a messy kill, blood was everywhere, and the cleanup was a bitch, but I will never forget the feeling of calmness that had swept over me after the deed was done.

I needed to kill, to fill whatever dark hunger was inside of me.

I felt my cock harden as I remembered my first. The blood, the thrill of pressing the knife against bare, soft skin, watching red ooze out in a thick line. There was nothing better than being in complete control, and conversely, nothing worse than losing it.

My hand went to grip my dick, and before I knew what I was doing, I was pumping along its length, jacking myself off in the shower. My eyes closed, and I breathed hard. It just wasn't the same when it was me doing it; to have someone else's hand, someone else's mouth around it? The best, especially if that person knew what they were doing.

Hips starting to buck, to sway along with the movement of my hand, I felt the pleasure growing inside, and I didn't bother trying to delay it. I knew Ed was probably in the kitchen, about done with dinner. Didn't want to keep him waiting too long.

It wasn't but two minutes later when I felt myself being pushed over the edge. Cum shot out of me, landing on the tile above the water spout, smudging as it seeped down onto the knob that controlled the temperature. I sagged back, washing off my hand in the water before turning it off.

Eh. I'll clean it up later.

Stumbling out of the tub, I grabbed a towel, drying myself off. My dick was still erect; it'd probably take a few minutes to get back to normal. I didn't bother putting on clothes before stepping out of the bathroom, walking down the hall as I rubbed the towel on my head, drying my black hair.

My looks, I'd been told on multiple occasions, were extremely high on the scale of attractiveness. I was over six foot, tall, compared to some men I supposed. Muscular because I had to be—how else could I overpower our chosen ones? I was, basically, the epitome of tall, dark, and handsome.

I dropped my towel on the backside of the couch, glancing to where Ed was in the kitchen, cooking some complicated dish that looked like it involved a million different ingredients. He wore clean clothes, and an apron above it all. Whatever meat he'd chosen to cook had been bloody, for his fingers were stained red.

Ed was not like me. A little shorter, along with having the looks of the stereotypical teenage heartthrob. You know the type—blonde hair, blue eyes, dimples that made girls and women of all ages swoon. Only now we were both in our thirties, and our skills involving manipulation had only grown.

"Had a fun shower?" Ed asked, glancing up over the island, where he worked to cut whatever meat into thin slices. He didn't even blink at my nakedness; it was not new to him. More often than not I was naked in this house. Clothes were just so…restricting.

And another thing to take off.

I grumbled an affirmative, reaching for the remote and turning up the volume. The nightly news was on, and the pretty newscaster was busy telling the weather for the next week, an awfully out of date green screen behind her.

Ed paused in his cutting, using his elbow to tap something on his phone, which sat off to the side. The damned man actually scrolled using his *elbow*. I couldn't even describe how stupid he looked.

"What are you doing?" I asked, not really caring.

"It's Tuesday," he said, as if it should be all I needed. It was not.

"What the fuck does it matter if it's Tuesday? You got some stupid ass TV show on later or something?" Truthfully, Ed was more normal than I was, because there weren't many things I enjoyed. Ed kept me grounded, kept me sane. Without him, I'd probably either be dead or in jail.

More like federal prison.

"Another article was released." Ed went on, reading directly from his phone, *"What makes a killer?"*

I tried to listen as he read the entire article out loud, so wrapped up in his own imagination I had to roll my eyes. Ed and his fucking fascination with the journalist. Whoever she was, she probably had an army of people like Ed wanting to meet her—and wanting to kill her.

When he was done, I said, "You've been stalking her articles for months."

"I know," Ed said, shrugging as he got back to cooking. "I think it's time."

Okay, at that I had to look at him. "You want to meet her? Ed, she's not a nameless woman on the street. She's published and probably well known in her town."

"I didn't say I wanted to kill her, just meet her. Maybe she writes about people like us because she is like us," Ed spoke, desperate hope evident in his tone. The bastard longed for another person to this duo, because apparently I wasn't enough.

I stretched my arms on the back cushion, lifting my legs and resting my feet on the coffee table. My dick was fully limp now. "And if she's disappointing?" I knew what the answer would be before I even asked the question. So why'd I ask? I couldn't say.

"Then I brainstorm and think of a way to kill her," Ed said simply.

Right. Because people like Ed, and by extension people like me, could never just leave someone alone.

"I have off tomorrow. I'm going to scope her out. Start at the Tribune, see if she's there."

I knew his ways. Ed was a master at finding people, even better at playing the normal card. Women and men alike flocked to his dimples and his charm, and once they realized they were in the spider's web, it was far too late.

"What's her name?" I asked.

"Stella Wilson."

This Stella Wilson had no idea the shitstorm heading her way. Ed might look pretty, but deep down, he was just as psychotic as I was. Stella Wilson was in for a world of hurt.

Chapter Three - Stella

I started my day off by taking a bubble bath. A weird time for a bath, but on days off, there was hardly anything I could think of to do. I'd probably stay in the bath for an hour until I was a prune, then make my way to the couch, where I'd flip on the TV and work on my next blog post. I was in the middle of writing posts about the most famous American serial killers. My next one was about Ted Bundy.

A knock on the bathroom door drew me out of my thoughts, and Callie walked in, wearing fishnet stockings, a short skirt, and a shirt that showed her midriff—which was flat, but still. I didn't need to see it, especially from the position I was in. I didn't need to know, for instance, she wasn't wearing underwear beneath the skirt and the fishnets.

Plus, I was naked and in the tub. Hadn't she ever heard of privacy? It was a good thing I had made enough bubbles to cover my private parts, otherwise I would've given her an earful about barging in.

Still, I did find it meaningful to say, "Why the hell aren't you wearing underwear?" I averted my eyes as she bent over the sink and ran a tube of red lipstick over her lips.

Callie was my best friend, but sometimes she could get a little…strange.

I was jealous of her, in a way. With her salon-highlighted brown hair, cut in layers to frame her heart-shaped face, not to mention her brown eyes that were much warmer and welcoming than mine, she was every man's dream. Plus, ever since middle school, when she'd blossomed and popped and grew every which way imaginable, I couldn't help but feel a tad insecure. My boobs were nothing like hers, even if, she swore to me a lot more than once, men didn't care as long they got boobs in general.

"I have a date today," she said with a smile. "I'm meeting John for lunch, and then we're seeing a movie." Callie puckered her lips in the mirror, as if practicing her *kiss me now* face. She had the sultry, seductive expression down pat since she was fifteen. The way she was dressed, she planned on doing a lot more than kissing with this John guy.

"Doesn't John have a job? Don't you?" I joked. Was this the first time I was hearing about John? I couldn't remember. Just went to show how good of a friend I was. Callie deserved better.

Callie put the red lipstick away, turning to lean on the counter as she stared down at me in the mess of bubbles. "What about you? You have any plans for today?"

Like a good friend, she always asked, and like a good friend, I always assured her I wouldn't be bored without her. I knew I dragged her down, because I wasn't as social as her, didn't have other friends like she did. Definitely had no boyfriends. It hurt to lie to her constantly, but I didn't want her worrying about me.

"Killian invited me out for drinks with the others. It's his birthday today," I said, not sure why I felt like sharing the whole thing. Now that I mentioned Killian's name, she'd always find a way to bring him up. It had taken her three months after the Christmas party to stop talking about him.

Callie grinned. "Killian, huh? Finally giving the fuckup another chance?" She was a fan of drunk proclamations of love, so the whole coming onto me thing hadn't nearly been as intense and frightening to her as it had been to me at the time.

"No, but it's something to do, isn't it?"

My friend couldn't argue with that logic. "Okay, but just remember, be safe. If you need any condoms—"

I instantly wanted to plug my ears. "Thanks, but I think I'll pass."

Callie shrugged. "Suit yourself. If you change your mind though, they're in the top drawer of my nightstand. I'll see you later. Feel free to text me updates—I'll probably be staying over at John's tonight, but I'm always down to crash a birthday party." She giggled before leaving me alone in my bath, finally.

Shit. I couldn't believe I'd spilled the beans to Callie. Somehow, my best friend always had a super easy time prying things like this from me. I wore everything on my sleeve when it came to her, and sometimes I wished I could be more of a closed book. Now I felt like I had to go tonight, so I wouldn't be a liar—and I so didn't want to.

After the water got cold and the bubbles popped, I got out of the bath and dried off. I called the office and got the address of the bar, along with the time. I was fully committed to going now, so after sitting and watching TV while typing out my next blog post, I chose my outfit.

A clean black shirt, sleeveless, along with jeans that were not ripped or discolored. I thought they were nice choices, but what did I know when it came to fashion? I was more of a lazy person when it came to dressing for the day. I was the one wearing yoga pants every day before and after work, even while running errands and going food shopping. Comfort over beauty.

I threw on my chosen outfit, did just the barest hints of makeup, and waited. Yeah…I was actually a really boring person, deep down. Boring, hardly any social skills, and weird. But I was okay with it, because I'd been this way my entire life. My hobbies and interests had always been viewed as odd by my parents, other classmates, and my coworkers.

Ironic that my articles about killers were the highest ranking and most viewed articles on the Local Tribune's website, wasn't it?

Before leaving the house, I grabbed my phone and my wallet. Purses were useless. I didn't have enough junk to lug around, so anytime I wasn't going to work, I just grabbed my wallet—a man's wallet, so it could fit in my back pocket—and my phone, which fit in the other. Having my hands free was not something I wanted to give up.

I locked the front door behind me with my key as I opened a new message. From my mom, asking if I was free anytime next week. Right. How the hell could I have forgotten? Bree, my little sister, was getting married, and I was the maid of honor. Cue the eye-rolling and the ugly dress montages. I had to meet them for the fitting, get measured so my maid of honor dress actually fit me. Not what I wanted to do, at all.

I texted back as I walked along the sidewalk. *I'll have to check my schedule and get back to you.* With any luck, that would be that, and my mom would drop it. Not only was I forced to go to this birthday thing for Killian, but I was also forced to think about my younger sister and how she was everything our parents ever wanted. I, on the other hand, was just one big disappointment.

Couldn't make it up, because it's true. Our parents put all of their effort into Bree. The minute I moved out, it was like I didn't exist anymore. It hurt, it hurt for a long time, because until then, I'd always thought my parents and I had a good relationship. I never got in trouble, always listened to their word like it was law. I got good grades and didn't do drugs or get pregnant.

All of my accomplishments, all of my effort—it meant nothing. Bree was twenty-two years old, got in trouble for drinking multiple times before she even turned eighteen, and yet *she* was the golden child. Not me. *Never* me.

No one ever chose me.

It wasn't like I wanted to be the center of their attention constantly. I wasn't that selfish or stupid, but parents were supposed to love their children equally, weren't they? How the hell did I get stuck with a family like this?

It didn't matter. I shouldn't think about it. I couldn't change it, so there was absolutely no point to it.

Sliding my phone into my back pocket, I swore to myself I would not glance at it again until tonight, when

I plugged it into the charger before bed. I would not give my mom the satisfaction of knowing I was hung up on her reply, or her attention. I was my own woman, damn it, and I was going to start acting like one.

I was…over an hour early to the bar. I was so lame. So ridiculously lame.

I sat at the counter, ordered a pop, and munched on the nuts, starving. I didn't eat today, I realized. I should've. It was funny how often I forgot to do the little things that kept you alive. Eating, sleeping. I was too lost in my own head and worries, I guess. Strange how some things were needed to survive, but so easy to forget.

The party, or whatever they were calling it, went as good as I expected. Once everyone showed up, it was all laughter and alcohol, everyone trading stories about Killian, who stood at the center of the group near the pool table, blushing—either from his strong drink or the stories his employees were telling. Right now, it was clear he was more like a friend than a boss.

I stood to the side of the group, sipping my pop. It was my…third refill? Alcohol wasn't my thing. I liked being in control of all of my senses, and I did not need my head to hurt or the world to spin. Even so, the group was a bit too loud. Too rowdy. My head was starting to hurt regardless.

Sandy stood beside Killian, wearing a tight blue dress, showing off a bit of leg. Every time she spoke, she made sure to laugh, causing her chest to jiggle and every straight male's eyes to move to her bouncing breasts, including Killian's. She'd touch his arm when she spoke, lean over the pool table too far when it was her turn to shoot. I found her antics annoying and desperate, but the others must not have felt that way.

I was an outsider among everyone—family, friends, coworkers. There was no place for me to belong.

Did I mind being a fly on the wall, even in my own life? Not really, but I didn't have the energy or the know-how to stand on my own. Living with Callie, being a journalist and a blogger—it was different than actually living.

What I was doing, it wasn't living. It was barely scraping by—but it's okay, because I never thought I'd be one of those people who lived until they were eighty or ninety.

Not saying I wanted to die young, but…

"Stella," Sandy called out to me, raising her glass after drinking a huge gulp of beer from it. Or was it considered a mug? I didn't know the semantics, because I wasn't a drinker, not like these people. Why the hell was I here again? "You're awfully quiet over there."

God, when people addressed my different-ness, I really felt my skin prickle in annoyance.

I leaned against the wall behind the pool table, forcing myself to smile at her words. It didn't matter whether or not she meant them how I took them; I was annoyed, and I didn't get annoyed easily. "I'm just watching the show," I said.

Sandy stunned more than one person as she slapped Killian on the ass and said, "Me too."

Killian, who was before then bending over to line up a shot, instantly straightened. "Sandy, that's inappropriate." His words slurred a bit, and I could tell he didn't really mean it.

"Is it my turn to slap the boss's ass?" Clive, the formatter of both the paper's printed form and the website, spoke up, raising his hand questioningly. His sarcastic quip caused the group to erupt in a fit of giggles, and I had to step away.

My drink was nearly gone anyway. Time for a refill. Or maybe I should just go.

After getting the bartender's attention and sliding him my glass, as I waited for my refilled cup, I was no longer alone at the bar. Killian had followed me after handing the pool cue to Clive. He set his glass on the counter, staring heavily at me.

A beat of silence before I said under my breath, "I shouldn't have come."

"Don't say that," he said. "I'm glad you're here, really. Ignore everything Sandy says—she's just going through a rough patch in her home life right now. Whether you're quiet or not, I want you here." As he spoke, he tentatively reached out to me, brushing my arm with his fingertips. Despite the alcohol, he sounded genuine. "You look good," Killian whispered, his eyes moving up and down. "With your hair not in a bun, I hardly recognize you." His fingers still touched me, and the longer I stood motionless, the more his palm brushed up against me.

I wasn't sure what he thought, but this wasn't an invitation to come onto me. This wasn't his second chance. I was not interested in Killian like that, even if he was cute. Looks were not everything.

"Killian," I spoke his name delicately, but I lost all sense of coolness when I quickly added, "please don't touch me." It came out in a rush, the words all mashed together like I couldn't wait to get them out. I winced at how much of a bitch I sounded like. It wasn't how I wanted to come off.

He was slow to pull his hand off my arm. His mouth thinned into a frown. "Right. I forgot you only like murderers."

"That's not—" *At all what I meant*, but I didn't get a chance to say it before he walked away, back to the group.

Well, that was a rude thing to do, drunk or not.

The bartender returned with my pop, and I thanked him without looking at him, still staring at Killian's back. I was measured in moving my stare to my carbonated beverage, getting lost in its warm brown color. It was a dark brown pop, the same color as my hair. I took a slow sip, wondering if I should just leave. I already paid for the drink—it came with unlimited refills, unlike all the alcohol the others were drowning themselves in—so what was the harm?

I mean, I came, I saw, I talked a little. What more was there? If I left now, I wouldn't be a liar to Callie.

Just as I was about to push myself off the stool and away from the counter, a smooth voice beside me said, "Don't take this the wrong way, but your boyfriend seems like a dick."

I hadn't expected anyone to talk to me, let alone call Killian my boyfriend, so it took me far too long to turn my head and meet the questioning blue eyes of the stranger who'd spoken. Older than me by a few years, maybe in his thirties. A square jaw with dimples that deepened when he smiled at me—and his smile, it was...a devastating kind of handsome. The kind of handsome I never knew was possible. Effortless. Short blonde hair, clean cut; there was nothing off-putting about him.

He was perhaps the most handsome man I'd ever seen, and I was not being dramatic.

"He's not my boyfriend," I finally said, once I got over the nerves this man's looks instilled in me.

"His loss then," the man said, grinning. Perfect white teeth, straight, not a single chip or stain. A flawless smile, dimples included.

I turned my head to look at him straight on, which allowed him to see my eyes. I'd found that if I didn't look at people, I couldn't see their reactions to my unique stare—it's why I hardly ever met strangers' eyes. But this man, whoever he was, I just had to look at him, had to see his reaction to my heterochromia.

Whereas most would've simply commented on how striking my eyes were, how pretty they were, he barely even blinked as he said, "Your eyes, I've never seen anything like them. I bet they get you into a lot of trouble."

I…wasn't quite sure what he meant by it. Was he flirting with me, or did he make a genuine observation? I spoke the truth, "I try my best to stay away from trouble."

A slight quirk in his mouth, not exactly a smile but a reaction I could not place. What I would give to be able to read minds, to know what he was thinking about in this moment.

"Oh," he said slowly, running his finger over the rim of his glass. "Then you'll probably want to steer clear of me." He watched me for a reaction, but I gave him none. "I'm Edward, by the way. Or Ed. Whichever one you prefer."

Despite myself, I was intrigued by this man. My thoughts of leaving the bar, my anger from Killian's accusation, faded in my mind. Front and center was Edward. Ed. The stranger beside me who somehow intrigued me beyond all belief. I was never curious about strangers, not really. But this man…there was something different about him. I could feel it.

I was drawn to it, to him.

"Stella," I said, knowing right then and there I could not leave. Not before I found out more about this man, not before I figured out why I was so drawn to him.

So I stayed, and I fully ignored the loud laughter and chatting coming from the pool table area. As night fell upon the world, the bar grew more packed, the tables and booths jammed with people, which only made it easier for me to ignore Killian and the rest of them. I never felt any texts from Callie, and I took it to mean she was having a good night with John.

"Stella," Ed spoke my name carefully, as if he'd never spoken a name like it before. "You don't seem like the type of person who belongs with those people."

I looked at him sharply. "What do you mean by that?"

"There's something about you that's different," he said. "Not bad, so please don't think I'm insulting you. You're just…different. It's hard to explain."

Studying him, I managed to say, "Funny you say that, because I get the same vibe from you. I feel like you're not like anyone else either." It was strange—I was almost smiling. This man, this stranger, made me want to *smile*.

We talked for a little while, but it was not long before my multiple refills of pop made me need to use the restroom. Using public restrooms, especially one in a bar, was not something I enjoyed, but I just couldn't seem to leave and go home. I liked this man. I liked the way he looked at me—different, and not only because of my eyes. I had to know more about him before the night ended.

"I have to use the restroom, excuse me," I said, sliding off the stool. Edward had scooted to the one beside me, and since then the others had been taken up by other people. "Save my seat?"

Edward gave me a smile, like it was so easy for him to do it. "As if I'd want to sit beside anyone else."

His reply made me…a bit self-conscious, actually. Was he trying to come on to me? I didn't know these things, because I didn't deal with guys that much, even though I was twenty-five. Callie always said I was a late bloomer. I wasn't saving myself for marriage or anything like that—I just…I could never connect with anyone. Not enough to want to sleep with them.

I made my way to the restroom in the back, pushing against the ladies' door and moving into the first stall, locking it behind me before I sat on the toilet. At least everything looked clean, relatively. For a bar. No puke or sticky floors.

It was as I was unrolling some toilet paper when someone else came into the bathroom, giggling drunkenly. The woman was not alone though, because as she passed my stall and went into the one beside mine, I saw another pair of feet following her.

I had to get out of here, fast. I didn't want to listen to anyone doing the dirty in a restroom in a damn bar. It stunned me to think some people found it a good time; I just found it nasty and gross. Not the sex part, but the restroom in a bar part.

The sounds of a belt buckle being undone made me hurriedly wipe and pull my pants up. I was just about to flush and make a run for it when I heard the woman talk, practically purring as she said, "I'm going to make you feel so good."

That was...Sandy's voice.

"Maybe we shouldn't..." The man spoke, and I instantly felt my stomach clench. Killian.

Killian and Sandy? What the hell? My mind had a hard time registering it. Sandy was nearly my mom's age, and Killian...I always thought he a thing for me. Which wasn't to say I owned him, but...it still felt like a betrayal of sorts.

"Shh," Sandy murmured, and I heard her getting to her knees.

Oh. So she was just going to give him a blowjob. That's all.

No—I couldn't deal with this. I couldn't. I couldn't sit here and listen to that shit. Hell, I didn't think I could even flush the toilet without one of them realizing it was me. Stupid, of course, because they'd probably seen me walk to the restroom in the first place.

And then, stupid, stupid me, I had a horrifying thought. What if Sandy saw me go to the restroom, and she dragged Killian back here on purpose? It wasn't like we were dating, so both Killian and Sandy were free to do whatever it was they wanted with whomever they wanted, but to make me listen? Hell no.

I exited the stall as quietly as I could, practically tiptoeing. I didn't even flush or wash my hands. Disgusting, but not as disgusting as listening to the wet sounds and the moans coming from the second stall.

Pushing out of the restroom, I paused in the back hall. It was much dimmer here than it was in the bar, and I could almost pretend to be home, alone, away from all of these people. How the hell was I supposed to ever look Sandy or Killian in the eye after that? How was I supposed to pretend I didn't hear their little exchange? I wasn't made for this, for being around people. I wanted to leave.

And I almost did.

I started from the hall, zigzagging through the people to get to the door, but then I saw Edward at the counter, and I instantly stopped. Halfway to the exit, I was close to being home-free, but then I'd leave him, and I'd never be able to dive into the reason why I felt so drawn to him.

No. You know what? Fuck Sandy and fuck Killian—not literally, of course, but metaphorically.

I was going to stay.

Chapter Four - Edward

Stella Wilson was not what I expected. Honestly, I wasn't sure what to expect. She was…pretty. Not in an overbearing way, but just pretty. How her dark brown hair was slightly messy, a little frizzy, like she tried to put herself together and couldn't quite get the hang of it. Her lips weren't the fullest, but they were shaped perfectly, her mouth still alluring in every way.

And, who could've ever imagined, her eyes. Her eyes were startling and unique and beautiful. I wasn't lying when I said they probably got her into trouble, and I bet nearly everyone she met made comments about them—which was why I didn't compliment her on them. It wasn't like she created her eyes herself. She was born with them. They were incredibly beguiling, but they did not make the woman behind them.

She was…awkward. Socially inept. Stella was the type of person to act cool and collected, even when she was lost in her own thoughts. She hardly showed expression on her face.

I liked her.

I liked her even before she opened her mouth to speak, before she looked at me with those crazy-colored eyes. Hell, I'd be lying if I said I didn't like her before meeting her—Lincoln was right. I was obsessed with her simply based on her articles.

But to finally put a face to the name, to see her trying to fit in with people who clearly didn't understand her, it made me want her that much harder. Stella was not like any woman I'd ever met before. She was more like Lincoln and me, I knew, just from our conversation before she went to the restroom.

There was a darkness inside of her, and I wanted to unleash it.

I also wanted to tie her to my bed and fuck her raw, but one thing at a time.

As I waited for her, I wondered whether Lincoln would like her. We shared everything, whether we wanted to or not. It was just how we did things. Our kills, our conquests, our appetite for destruction. We were both hungry, carnal beasts. Would Stella be able to handle us both?

Hmm. I was getting too far ahead of myself. I wasn't even certain she liked *me*.

That would be the first step.

Patience was not one of my virtues, and I found myself growing annoyed at everyone around me. The nonstop laughter, the clinking of glasses on tables, the munching of nuts by the men beside me. There were too many people in the world. Lincoln and I were doing it a favor by trimming its numbers.

Finally, after what felt like a lifetime, I saw Stella emerge from the hall in the back. I watched her with interest as she headed straight for the door, like she was going to leave. Her face looked...distraught. Almost. She stopped about halfway to the door, slowly turning her head to look at me.

I didn't want her to leave. I'd just found her—she wasn't getting away from me that easily.

Just as I started to think of ways to get her to stay, whether I'd have to follow her home or not—I would find out eventually where she spent her nights alone and asleep—Stella came to me, deciding against leaving. Still, I was a little hurt, so as she slipped onto the stool beside mine, I muttered, "Don't stay on my account."

"Sorry," she said, not sounding too sorry at all. "I'm just…" Stella trailed off, glancing over her shoulder, at her group of coworkers, still hanging around the pool table. I noticed then two of them were gone—the one who said she only liked murderers, and the middle-aged woman who reeked of desperation.

Was that why she looked uneasy? Did she see them hooking up?

I didn't even really know the woman beside me, and yet I grew angry on her behalf. It was clear it troubled her, and I didn't want to see her pretty face distraught, even if it was only a little.

"Hey," I spoke softly, "you doing okay? Did something happen?" I hated playing dumb. It was not one of my strong suits. I always knew more than I let on, and this woman—she might have everyone else fooled, but I could see right through her.

She craved the darkness. She craved it and didn't even realize it. Luckily for her, I was here now, and I would show her just how beautiful and unrelenting the darkness could be.

Stella shook her head. "No, I'm fine. It's nothing." She preferred to keep her thoughts and her secrets to herself, which was fine…I didn't mind prying them out of her. I planned on doing much more to her tonight.

Though I knew all about her, I still found myself asking, "So, Stella, what do you do for a living?" I couldn't exactly tell her I already knew what she did, and that I'd pretty much followed her coworkers here after stalking her place of work all day, hoping she'd be here. It was pure luck she came on her own, I knew.

"I work for the Local Tribune," Stella said, reaching for her glass, but she didn't drink it. Did she worry whether or not I put something in it while she was gone? Women were paranoid these days, for good reason. There was always someone willing to take advantage of them, especially when they were at their weakest point. When I took a woman to bed, I made sure she always wanted it.

Killing…well, that was another story.

"The paper?" I asked. "What do you write?" She wrote about killers, had a blog about them too. I had read every single article this woman had ever written. I even went into her backlog from years ago and read the blog articles she wrote while she was in high school.

This woman had been obsessed with the darkness for a long time.

I couldn't blame her, though. I liked the darkness too. It was more a home to me than anything, more a parent to me than my actual parents. Lincoln and I weren't related in the strictest of sense, but we were like brothers in that way. We were both so immeasurably fucked up, and we reveled in it.

Stella took her time to answer me, "I write about killers. Serial killers, specifically."

I nodded along, pretending to just now realize it. "You know, I think I actually have read some of your stuff. The online articles. You're a good writer."

Compliments were not things I gave freely, yet here I was, giving them to this woman. This pretty, broken woman who put on a mask anytime she was in public.

What would she look like beneath her mask? What thoughts raced inside that head of hers?

She shrugged my compliment off—which she wouldn't have done, if she'd known how rare they were. "Only when I'm writing about things that interest me. I think my boss is getting tired of my articles, though." Stella rubbed her bare arms, as if she was cold. "Even though he was the one who said I could write whatever I want."

"He lets you write what you want for every paper?"

"At first, no. It was just for the Wednesday edition. But when he started to see the higher traffic to the website, he did."

I could not stop looking at her, checking her out. Every time she moved, it was a calculated movement. She was socially awkward, but it could all very well be an act. I knew these things, because I used to be like her, years and years ago, before I'd met Lincoln and fallen into his family business.

What was this woman hiding?

"Why do you find them so interesting?" I asked as I was busy studying the way she kept kicking the bottom of her own stool absentmindedly.

Stella was lost in her own thoughts. She looked at me suddenly, her blue eye drawing my attention. "What?" Almost like she hadn't heard a word I'd said.

Her eyes were…God, they were fucking amazing. The most beautiful set of eyes I'd ever seen, easily, hands down. The more I looked at them, the easier it was for me to get lost in them. The blue one especially.

Its color was lighter, purer than my own, not a single bit of brown in it. And her brown eye—a light, warm amber. I could definitely see how people might label her special only because of her eyes, but I knew she was much more than her rare gaze.

"Serial killers," I said. "What about them do you find so interesting?"

She was slow to shrug, apparently not as verbose or eloquent as her articles would suggest. "I don't know. I guess I find everything about them interesting. I don't think there's a single boring serial killer out there."

"What got you into first writing about them?" I had to know more, had to dive into her head. If I could pry her open and see for myself what made her tick—without killing her—I would in a heartbeat.

This woman...I needed her. I needed her right fucking now.

"I remember growing up, hearing about them. One was caught a few cities away from my parents' house, and the news coverage was constant for the next few months, and even after the trial. I just...I felt..." Stella trailed off, running a hand through her hair as she straightened her back. "I just knew."

I asked how long she'd been working for the Tribune, whether she went to college. The usual stuff. Her parents had paid for college, I found out, and she majored in psychology. She had wanted to know more about the criminal mind, but her university's program was more about the data collection rather than the individual subject. So, somehow she wound up here, a few hours away from her hometown and a couple more away from her college.

Everything I asked of her, Stella told me without hesitation, as if there was not a thing called oversharing with a stranger. I found it refreshing, because most women liked to play coy, or give roundabout answers that weren't really answers. Stella was unique in more ways than one.

I learned she shared a house with a single roommate, her best friend from high school. Callie was her name, and Stella spoke of her fondly. It was the one time her face truly lit up, and she damn near almost smiled as she told me some of her friend's antics. Her friend, it sounded like, had never moved on from the boy crazy phase from their young adult years.

What I would give to see this woman smile. That, and see her naked under me. I couldn't help but wonder what it would take to get her to come home with me. Lincoln worked the second shift, so he wouldn't get home until after midnight. Stella and I could have the whole house to ourselves, and get to know each other *very* well…

"So," I said, doing my best to sound normal and not overly curious, "since that prick isn't your boyfriend…" She stared at me, as if confused as to where my question was going. "Are you single, then?"

Stella's gaze fell, and I couldn't help but wonder where her eyes landed. "I am," she whispered, dragging the two words out for an eternity, like she was afraid to say them. Like she knew, deep down, her answer was all I needed to officially make her mine.

The truth was, I wouldn't give a single shit if she had a boyfriend. No one could possibly treat her well enough. No one could ever appreciate her like I could. I would worship the ground she walked on, make her smile, make her feel things no one else had made her feel before. Open her eyes to the wonders of the world, and to the beauty of darkness. True darkness.

This woman…she wrote about killers, but she'd never stared one in the face before tonight.

When I only stared at her, Stella asked, "Is this when you say I'm in luck, or something cheesy like that?" She sounded almost hopeful. Everything about her was…almost. Almost, but not quite. She was not whole.

"I'm in the market for more than just a girlfriend," I said, leaning closer to her. She didn't lean away, which only excited me. Maybe I was getting to her after all—one step closer to actually being inside of her. She would not look so emotionless while I was pounding away at her.

She played my game by asking, "What are you looking for, Edward?"

Edward. She liked my full name best. I liked how it sounded on her tongue.

What else could she do with that tongue?

"I need a partner," I said, keeping the fact I already had a partner in Lincoln to myself. One thing at a time. I didn't want to scare her off before getting her naked and alone. "A partner in crime, a partner in bed—" I was going to say more, but she interrupted me.

Ah, so the woman had some balls of her own; she just chose when to show them.

Stella matched my posture, leaning closer to me. A twinkle danced in her eyes, both of them, almost like she was excited. "What kind of crime are you getting into?" A soft, gentle, near nonexistent smile grew on her lips. "Should my next article be about *you*?"

Oh, my. How right she was, and how badly she tempted me. I wanted to throw her over my shoulder and take her home this instant—or have at her here and now—but I held back. It was hard to keep my hands off her, and I felt the familiar stirring of my dick in my pants.

"You have no idea of the things I could show you," I whispered. Her face was inches from mine, and I could smell her soap. Lavender. Her skin looked soft, too. Without a blemish. No acne scars, no beauty marks or moles. No wrinkles. The closer I got to her, the more perfect she looked.

How flawless would she look when her legs were spread under me? What sounds would she make as she squirmed? My mind danced. Would she enjoy being tied up, or would she like to take charge and for once be the one dominating me? My dick perked up even more at the thought. I never thought I was the kind of man to submit to anyone, but maybe to Stella...

Stella didn't move away from me. She murmured, so quiet it was hard to hear her, even with our closeness, "And what things are those?" If she wanted me to be more specific, I would gladly oblige.

"Maybe we should start with the things I would do to you." I moved a hand, drawing a finger tentatively along her cheek, watching as she shivered at my touch. Fuck. I needed this woman, and I needed her now. "First thing, I'd take you home and make you take off your clothes. Then I'd tie you up and spread your legs."

Her breath caught in her throat as my finger ran over her lips. Still, she did not pull away. She wanted more; I could see it in her eyes.

"I would make every part of you mine," I whispered, stopping myself from leaning forward and taking her lips right here and now. I couldn't, because if I got started, I wouldn't be able to stop. "Claim you as mine with my mouth and my hands, before I make that sweet hole of yours wet with my dick—" Speaking of my dick, it was rock hard now. So much for trying to keep it low key while in public.

Stella didn't give me a chance to say more—and I definitely could've kept going. I had a long list of things I'd do to her, and I could get extremely detailed. No, the woman surprised me when she said, "Let's go."

Oh, fuck. This woman had no idea what was headed her way, but I'd make sure she enjoyed every last part of it.

Chapter Five – Stella

As Edward quickly paid his tab and grabbed my hand, leading me out of the bar, I was stunned at myself. Why did I say that? I wasn't the kind of person who went home with a stranger, let alone a person who let a stranger talk to me like that.

I would be a liar if I said it didn't make me warm in certain places, though. A bad liar. And I couldn't help but feel connected to Edward in the weirdest way, almost like I knew him. Almost like we'd met before, in another life. Not that I believed in reincarnation, but…if fate existed, it had to have played a hand in our meeting tonight.

Everything felt right.

We left the bar, and I didn't even look to see if Killian was watching. I didn't care. If he could have some fun time with one of his employees—with *Sandy*—then I could do whatever I wanted, too. We weren't dating, we weren't together. We were both adults free to make our own decisions.

I might've just made the worst decision of my life, going home with a strange man who looked like he could bend me in half and break me, but I was so suddenly very tired of playing the good girl. I wanted to be bad, and I wanted to be bad with Edward.

He brought me to his car, not even asking about mine. I wasn't even sure where he lived, where he was taking me. I supposed he could be a serial killer or some other kind of criminal—he had seemed very unperturbed by my fascination with them. Maybe he was taking me back to his place just to make me his next victim.

I…would again be a liar if I said the possibility didn't appeal to me, as twisted as it was.

It wasn't like I had a death wish—I didn't want to die. It would just be fitting, in the grand scheme of things, if that's how I went.

As Edward got into the driver's side and started his car, driving us to God knew where, I started to wonder. If he tried to kill me, would I fight back? Not only was I weaker than him, but also smaller. He had every advantage. Plus, I'd never once taken a self-defense class, in spite of my parents' guidance. *Gotta learn to protect yourself.* Bullshit.

If a killer wanted me, he could take me. I probably wouldn't be the victim he wanted, or the one he was hoping for, but…oh well, right?

I debated on asking where Edward lived, whether or not I should text Callie to let her know I had gone home with a random stranger, but I kept quiet, and I didn't once reach for my phone. I would have stories to tell her in the morning, presuming I lived through the night.

I rolled my ankles as I watched the city blocks pass by. From the look of it, we were heading out of town and into the next city over. Huh. Had to be fate to meet Edward at the bar, considering there had to be other places he could've gone closer to home.

Neither of us said much during the thirty-minute car ride. I shot side glances to him every few minutes, finding he was busy staring at the road ahead. His focused face was cute—a weird thought for me, because I didn't often gush about guys' looks. Then again, never before had I ever wanted to be so free with myself and my body. Not even on the double dates Callie had set up numerous times to try to get me out of my shell.

Edward pulled us into the garage of a quaint, two-story house. It looked relatively updated, well-kept. As he shut the car off and got out, closing the garage door behind us, I couldn't help but wonder if he owned or rented the place. What did he do for a living? A question I should've asked him earlier, but he was too zeroed in on me to give me a chance to ask anything about him.

I followed him into the house, coming into a clean, modern kitchen. Loads and loads of subway tile, painted cabinets, the whole shebang. It was a pretty place; put mine to shame.

"Bedroom's this way," Edward said, heading down the hallway and up the stairs, passing the living room, where a sectional and a recliner sat across from a huge TV that had to be at least seventy inches. He took his entertainment very seriously.

I trailed after him, a strange feeling growing inside of me. Was I nervous? Was that what this was? I shouldn't be, because Callie did things like this all the time, as did pretty much every woman on TV. This was normal, wasn't it? I wasn't sure. I didn't know. I was not the most normal woman around.

His bedroom was not the only bedroom upstairs; we passed a rather dark and gloomy room before we reached his. Luckily his roommate didn't seem to be home. Edward stepped into his bedroom first, flicking on the light, stepping aside to let me enter. I spun in a circle, studying the decorating. Simple, elegant. Clean. Light colors on everything, even the bedspread. The headboard was the darkest thing, a deep mahogany.

As he closed the door, Edward's eyes ate me up, more intrusive than anyone else's stare had ever been. He did not linger on my eyes, which was nice. I was more than my pretty eyes; at least I thought so.

"Take off your clothes," he said, getting right to the point. Edward stepped forward, placing me between the foot of the bed and him. "Take them off, or I'll rip them off you." Spoken not as a threat but as a promise—a promise that made my heart flutter.

Was I crazy for finding his dominant tone the most attractive thing I'd ever heard and his serious expression the sexiest thing I'd ever seen?

I couldn't disobey him, even if I wanted to—and I didn't want to. I would give in to any demand he made of me, regardless of what it was. This man had me wrapped around his finger so quickly I had whiplash in the best of ways.

I found myself turning, giving him my back, but he stopped me with a low chuckle. The sound sent tingles down my spine. It was almost a cruel chuckle, cold but not quite. I loved the sound.

"It's adorable that you think I'm going to let you take them off without looking at me," he said. "Turn and face me, and then take them off, *slowly*. Watching is my second favorite part."

Not sure what he meant by it, I was measured in facing him again, meeting his blue stare. My fingers toyed with the bottom hemline of my shirt, and I sluggishly drew my arms up as I clutched the fabric. Up and over my head the shirt went, messing up my hair a bit, but my hair was always messy. Messy hair and a messy mind.

When my shirt fell to the floor, Edward nodded once. "Good," he said, though his tone wasn't exactly praising me. "Now your boots, and then your pants."

I bent down to unzip my boots, sliding them off one by one, and then I went to undo the button on my jeans. Within a minute, my jeans were on the ground with my shirt and boots, and I stood there in nothing but my underwear and my bra. Never wore socks—wasn't a fan, even on cold winter days.

I felt…a bizarre mixture of turned on and apprehensive. The way he looked at me, at my body, made me feel warm all over, but I couldn't help but also feel anxious. What if this was all a game? What if he didn't like my body or me at all? If this was some sick, cruel joke, I didn't think I'd be able to take it.

But when he stepped closer, one of his hands moving to touch my side, all of my doubt and worry faded instantly. Edward's grip was firm and strong, possessive in a way it shouldn't be, considering we just met tonight. What was even odder, however, was the acceptance I felt. If he was going to be possessive, I might as well be possessed.

No one had ever wanted me like that before—at least no one I would've been okay with.

Edward, well, I didn't know him, but I felt like I did. I was drawn to him in a way I'd never been drawn before. Such a cliché thing to admit, but there it was, plain as day, out in the open.

He could possess me all he wanted, could look at me like his prized possession all he wanted. I was not an object, but he could own me and use me however he saw fit.

And then, just like that, Edward stepped back, his hand sliding off me as he said, "Next. I'll leave the choice up to you." How kind of him.

I reached behind me, never breaking eye contact with him, and unhooked my bra, letting the sheer black cups fall to the floor beside me. My chest inhaled deeply, and I didn't need to look to know my nipples were already hard, either from the sudden change in temperature or the fact I was turned on. Maybe a mixture of both.

I wanted this man more than I'd ever wanted anything in my entire life.

Tonight was full of firsts.

As his gaze ate me up, I slid a finger between my underwear and my hip. Soon enough, it was on the floor too, and I stood before Edward stark naked, a bit chilly, and fully ready for whatever was going to come next.

It was almost like someone had taken over my body. This wasn't me. I would never strip for a stranger or go to his house without letting someone know where I was. Would I? I guessed I never had the opportunity before, or the inclination to do any of it.

"Get on the bed, on your back" was Edward's next command, and I all too willingly did as I was told.

The bed was cushioned and comfortable beneath me, and I rested my head on the mound of pillows in front of the headboard. I was showing Edward parts of me I'd never showed anyone else, and the night was far from over. It was a good thing I'd been on the pill for a few years, largely thanks to my mom's insistence.

Edward crawled over me, still clothed, though he had taken off his shoes. He leaned over me, grabbing my left wrist and hoisting it to the corner of the bed, where a rope sat, currently unused but waiting. He tied me down, wrist after wrist, expertly, and I couldn't help but wonder how many times he'd done this before.

How many other women had been in the same position I was in now? The thought of Edward with other woman was…not something I should think about, but my mind wandered all the same, both in misplaced jealousy and sick curiosity. Had they come just as willingly as I did?

It didn't matter. The other women weren't here now. I was, and I had to remember that. Right now it was just Edward and me.

When both of my wrists were tied up, Edward brought his face to mine. "Normally I like to tie your ankles too, but we'll save it for next time," he said, his hands moving down my arms and across my collarbone.

I couldn't help but tense at his touch—his hands were a little rougher than I expected them. Whatever he did, he used his hands a lot. I did find it interesting he thought there would be a next time…though who the hell was I trying to kid? This man had me basically a slave to him on the first night. If he wanted me again, I'd come running.

This was so unlike me, it was almost ridiculous. I never once thought I'd give myself to a total stranger, never thought I'd ever go home with anyone. Hell, I'd known Killian for a few years when he came onto me at the Christmas party, and while I found him decently attractive, there was nothing between us.

Edward was another story. I'd only met him hours ago, and I felt closer to him than I felt to anyone before. Physically, mentally, sexually. I wanted him to do every little dirty thing he could think of tonight. Such a strange admission, coming from me. Almost like I wasn't myself. Like I was two separate people, sharing a body.

Like the good, quiet me had kept the bad Stella from emerging all these years, and now she was here, ready to rock the world and get rocked in return.

Oh, yes. Bad Stella was here, and I wasn't about to let her go anywhere.

Chapter Six - Stella

Edward lowered his head, pressing his lips against my throat, kissing me in a deceivingly gentle manner. This man—with ropes permanently attached to the four posts of his bed, I knew he was wilder than his put-together appearance would suggest. Just how wild was he? I'd find out soon enough.

His hands brushed my chest, his fingers grazing over my nipples, tweaking and pulling at them, eliciting sounds from me I had never made before. I didn't want him to stop, even if it was a little painful. Maybe it was just new.

I didn't expect this to be a fairytale encounter, so when his mouth went down instead of up to my lips, I didn't whine or groan. I wanted to see just what his mouth could do.

Edward's mouth went to the nearest nipple, his teeth grazing the risen pebble, his tongue dancing in swirls around it. I found myself arching my back and spreading my legs under him; a natural response to such a teasing sensation.

I wanted more, and more I would get.

His mouth abandoned my nipple. "You're a greedy one, aren't you?" Edward asked in a hushed whisper after I'd spread my legs. Had he not told me he wanted them spread before him? I couldn't exactly help what my body was doing—it was a stranger to me at this point. "Good, because tonight I'm feeling generous."

As he spoke, his hands traversed down my body, over my flat stomach. One of them dug into my hip while the other…while the other went someplace no hand had gone before. Not even my own.

I'd never seen the point in touching myself. Masturbation was not something that ever popped into my head as I was growing up, even as a teenager. Never really felt the need or the urge to have a release. But tonight, tonight all of that changed, and it was something I wanted more than anything.

His fingers slid against me, curving alongside my body, caressing the most sensitive part of me. I let out a moan; it came from me before I could stop it—and I would've stopped it too, because I didn't want Edward to know just how much I'd truly given into him.

He worked me with ease, like playing an instrument he'd been around for years, something he'd mastered long ago. Edward was my maestro, my fiddler and my master. He put most of his focus on a nub of pink, soft skin at the apex, watching me squirm and moan all the while. I didn't feel self-conscious; maybe I should have. This was not something normal women did, not with strangers.

But I didn't care. Tonight, caring about what normal women did was the last thing on my mind. I surrendered.

"You are so wet for me," Edward murmured, his blue gaze rising to mine. "You feel amazing. I can't wait to be inside of you, to feel you all around me." His words were dirty, and they made me only want him more, which I didn't even think was possible. I was already a slave to his will; what more did the man want from me?

He dipped a finger in me, just one, which was probably more than enough, since the only other thing that had ever been inside my vagina was my gynecologist at my yearly checkup. It didn't hurt; on the contrary, I hardly felt it. I wanted more down here, more to make me feel something.

As if reading my mind, Edward stuck another digit in, and he lowered his mouth to my apex. His tongue flicked out as his fingers worked me, moving along me in just the right way. My back arched again, and my eyes closed. I couldn't sit up and watch his face between my legs. It was too much.

I lost myself in what he did to me. The truth was, he could've pulled out a knife right then and there, and I wouldn't have even blinked to stop him, even if my wrists weren't tied up. Edward had me right where he wanted me, and I relished every single tingle of pleasure that coursed through my body thanks to his tongue and his fingers.

Really, I should thank all the women who'd been here before me, because without them, Edward would've had no practice. To get to a skill level like this took practice; I wasn't naive enough to think otherwise.

My body started to tense, my toes clenching and my fingers curling into fists. Something built inside of me, spiraled and grew until it was undeniable, until the pleasure exploded in my core, washing over me like a tidal wave of ecstasy, bliss shot directly into my body thanks to his hard work. I moaned loudly, unable to stop myself.

As Edward slowly withdrew his fingers from me, I wondered: was that an orgasm? Was that why I felt still a little tingly, even after the sensation was gone? I felt like I could have another one. I suddenly understood my sex-crazed best friend. All this time, Callie had known where it was at.

Edward lifted his head, saying, "The first of many I plan on giving you tonight." The way he said it, so matter-of-factly, made me shiver all the more. This man's power over me was insane, and it didn't make sense, but I was over fighting it.

He pushed himself off the bed, standing at the foot of it, his gaze lingering between my legs, which still ached for his touch and his mouth. *More*, my body screamed, *give me more*. Edward started to take off his clothes, and swiftly my body ached for something else.

His body was…more impressive with the clothes off. Edward had muscles, that much I'd already known, but the extent of which I had no idea until I looked at his naked body. The veins bulging in his arms, his defined pectoral muscles, the six pack sitting on his stomach below his belly button and the V-shape that led to his well-hung manhood. It did not surprise me to see his dick standing ready, hard and erect, ready for the next step.

I was literally going to lose my virginity to a stranger, but I didn't care one bit.

Before I could blink, he was on top of me again, leaning his forehead against mine. Edward said nothing, but I felt his hand move between us and position the head of his dick against me. I breathed in, holding the breath in my lungs, not sure what I should expect. His dick was longer and thicker than the fingers he'd stuck in me. Would this hurt? Was I not ready? We were about to cross the point of no return.

He must've seen my trepidation, for he whispered, "Relax, Stella. I'll make it feel good, I promise."

I didn't see how he could promise such a thing, but there was really no room to argue. He pushed inside of me slowly, as if being careful with me. I suppose I appreciated it, but it wasn't like he knew this was my first time, and I wasn't about to admit to him I was a virgin prior to this. How embarrassing.

Edward let out the sexiest groan a man could ever utter when he was fully inside of me, his length filling me up completely. It might've hurt a bit at first, more of an uncomfortableness really, but as he started to thrust his hips, dragging himself in and out of me, the discomfort faded and I was able to focus on the warm body above mine.

God, how badly I wanted to touch him. To hold him and feel his chest grunt against mine as he thrust into me. But I couldn't, because I was tied up and restrained. It was almost like I was an unwilling participant in this, and I couldn't help but wonder if it helped him get off, knowing I was restrained beneath him. Of course, I was the last person alive who had the right to judge anyone, so I let it go.

I let it go because I was enjoying being tied up just as much as he liked being in charge.

Edward kept a steady pace, almost like he was trying to drag it out. Again, I couldn't blame him—I didn't want this to end either. It felt too good to end so soon, too right. Fate had to have had a hand on us meeting tonight, because I never would've done this with any random stranger.

Edward and I…we were alike in more ways than one.

I was so lost in Edward—and by extension, he was so lost in me—we didn't hear anything beyond the bedroom.

Unfortunate, because soon we weren't alone.

Another man barged in the room, working to undo the top button on his dark uniform. His hair was black and cut close to the sides, a bit longer on top, and his eyes were a dark brown, practically black. His gaze landed on Edward and me, and he didn't even act surprised.

I couldn't even smack Edward on the back, couldn't seem to find my voice to alert him to the other man's presence. The other man, I swiftly saw the badge on his belt, was a goddamn *cop*.

If Edward could stop thrusting inside me, I could probably find my voice and warn him we were about to be arrested or something, but he wouldn't stop. He didn't care. And, I realized, neither did the cop. Instead of reacting how any sane person would've reacted to walking in on two people having sex, the dark haired man continued to unbutton his shirt, his gaze taking in every aspect of our positions.

Me, tied up and under Edward. Edward, pummeling me, the slick sounds of my vagina rising in the air.

Oh, God.

The cop wasn't even stunned. Was this his roommate? Did they…do this all the time? I didn't know what to think. Everything about sex was still kind of new to me—not to mention the instant attraction I'd felt for Edward. Should I turn away from the cop and look in the other direction? Should I pretend he's not even there? It was what Edward was doing.

As if sensing my confusion, Edward whispered, "Hey, just focus on me right now, Stella." He pressed his nose against my cheek, adding, "On me, and how wet you are. Come for me again."

It wasn't like I could orgasm on command.

I wanted to bare my teeth. I wanted to tell him I wasn't just some doll, but the annoyance inside of me faded almost instantly as I did what he instructed me to do. Focused on him, like he was the only other person in the room. Felt his length glide in and out of me. His hands went to my throat, as if he was going to choke me, and a thrill raced through me. Other man in the room or not…I liked it just as rough as Edward did.

The second time I came, I came to an audience with fingers curling around my neck.

Chapter Seven – Lincoln

I couldn't believe he got her, and I couldn't believe he was already fucking her. When I came home and headed up the stairs, the last thing I thought I'd walk into was Ed with the journalist. I heard the moaning, so I knew he'd be with someone, but the journalist he'd been obsessed with for the last few months? The man worked fast.

After barging into his bedroom, more curious than anything, I couldn't help but stare at her. Tied up, her pale skin all sweaty and flushed, she was a sight for sore eyes. Beautiful in the way all prey was when they were helpless and under Ed's and my control.

Stella could not stop staring at me, which I couldn't exactly blame her, I supposed. If Ed hadn't told her about me, about our…shared activities, well—of course she'd be a little freaked out. Who wouldn't? Nearly everything Ed and I did was considered taboo to society. Our shared conquests included.

I continued to take off my uniform, even after Ed told her to focus on him, watching as he grabbed her throat. His back glistening in sweat, he pounded into her with a sudden fierceness; Ed always had to be in utter control when he came. It was something I understood, because control was not something ever easily given, especially for people like us.

From my position, I could tell she was a small thing. Maybe five feet tall. Not an ounce of muscle on her and no fat to be seen. If anything, she was on the skinner side. It was like this woman hardly ate. When Ed's obsession with her died—and it surely would, because they always did—she would not put up any fight. A kindergartener could overpower her. Brown hair, thin face—she was pretty, though.

And then, when her body shook with pleasure—the exact same moment Ed's back tensed and he let out a guttural moan—I saw it. Or them, I should say. He forced her head to turn, burying his face in her neck as he slumped over her, spent for only the moment, and I saw her eyes.

One a bright, vibrant blue, so deep and pure it put the color of the sky to shame. The other was a neutral brown, both cold and warm at the same time. It was like staring at two different people, the colors so vastly different from each other.

I didn't like them. I didn't like them at all.

I shed my uniform piece by piece, eventually standing there naked, my dick hard. It didn't take much for me to get excited, and watching Ed have his way with his obsessions was one of them.

The question was, though, did Ed tell his newest flower he liked to share?

We shared everything, Ed and I. We've shared everything with each other for years now, and I didn't see it stopping anytime soon. Ed needed to be in control, whatever animal lurked inside of him had to be on top, but on the flip side, the animal had other cravings too. He had to watch, which was fine with me, because I liked a captive audience just as much as the next. Sometimes he wanted us to take them together; I was down for anything.

No matter how much he liked them, he always grew bored of them too, and then we had a different sort of fun with them. I would be lying if I said I didn't look forward to getting rid of his obsessions. There was just something so indescribably amazing about watching life vacate someone's eyes while feeling their warm blood seep on your hands. Oh, yes. There were some days I liked killing more than I did sex.

Tonight, I wasn't sure which one I was feeling more. This woman's fucking eyes were creeping me the fuck out. I wanted to pluck them out of her skull so she couldn't stare at me anymore. Would Ed stop me if I tried?

Probably. She was still shiny and new to him, so I would wait. Soon enough, I knew, we'd get to kill her anyway, whether it was tomorrow or a week from now.

Ed pulled out of her, his dick still semi-erect and dripping with cum and her slick. He stood, running a hand through his hair before turning to me, grinning. He looked like a boy when he smiled, with his fucking dimples and his innocent face. Who would ever guess that behind those sapphire eyes sat a psychopath waiting to emerge?

"So you got her," I said, glancing beside us.

The woman's legs were still spread; I could see white cum dribbling from her sex. A familiar ache crept up my balls. The sight was anything but a turn off. I liked sharing just as much as Ed did.

"I didn't tell her about you," Ed said, moving to look at her.

I held back a laugh. That much was obvious, based on the look on her face when I walked into the room. I had to give credit where credit was due though—she kept her legs spread, even though Ed hadn't tied down her ankles. She either didn't care we were looking at her, didn't care there were two naked men less than five feet from her, or she was trying hard not to move, pretending not to listen to our conversation.

"Maybe you should," I said. "Because I'm getting drained tonight, one way or another."

Ed nodded, not arguing with me. He returned to the bed, but instead of crawling on top of her, he moved beside her, running his hands through her hair, forcing her to look at him with those weird eyes. "I'm afraid I did keep something from you," he murmured, his voice sickeningly sweet. You caught more flies with sugar, and all that shit—something I hated.

Instead of freaking out, instead of saying anything remotely normal, Stella said, "I can see that."

Of course. With those fucking eyes, why the hell would she act normal? This woman...I hadn't even been in the same room with her for more than five minutes, and I already knew she wasn't normal, creepy eyes aside.

"This is Lincoln," Ed continued, gesturing to me. As if I needed any introduction, like she hadn't yet noticed me. "Lincoln and I...we share everything." His fingers moved along her jawbone, up her cheek, a disgusting display of affection. It was something I knew Ed was good at, making the prey caught in the web believe they weren't in danger.

A beat before Stella whispered, "You want to share me." It wasn't a question, more like a statement. She knew that's exactly what Ed wanted. She was smart, I could tell, even if it didn't take a rocket scientist to know that's where he was headed with this.

Ed gave her a slow nod. "I do, and I want to watch." He left it at that, waiting for her to say something.

"And if I say no?" Stella asked, to which Ed probably had a sweet sentimentality ready to go, but I had enough.

I moved to the foot of the bed, gripping her ankles hard. The woman didn't even flinch, hardly looked at me, which only further angered me. If she wanted to play games, I would be more than happy to call her bluff. "If you say no, I'll fuck you anyway. I'll fuck you until you say yes."

Something passed over her blue eye, clouded its depths. "You're angry. Why?"

I practically growled. As if she fucking cared. "I'm always angry," I muttered, crawling over her, my hands sliding up her legs. I watched her reaction as I touched her, harder than I knew Ed had touched her. Out of the two of us, I liked it rougher, a bit more violent.

Violence was like my fucking middle name.

How Stella looked at me then, the glimmer of acceptance in her freaky gaze, how she barely even looked at Ed, who cooed and cawed on her side, smoothing down her hair and generally being tender— I hated it. I hated her. Who the hell was she to look at me like that? To judge me? Oh, the woman had no idea just how bad I could really be.

"Fine," she whispered, sounding almost bored. Emotionless. As if she didn't care either way. "Then go ahead." Resigned, almost.

She wanted to play the cold, distant bitch? That was just fine with me. I didn't need her participation; the damned restraints always got in the way of that anyway. All I needed was her sweet pussy.

I wanted to make this bitch scream.

Grabbing myself, I set my tip right against her hole, still oozing with spent cum. She'd be leaking with mine soon. I pushed inside of her, grunting as I filled her up. I was longer than Ed, a bit thicker, too. She did her best not to move as I rammed inside, but she did let out a soft moan, almost like she wanted more.

So the distant, cold bitch was all an act, was it? It didn't matter. I'd fill her up with my cock and my cum, make it so she hurt when she walked. This woman wasn't my obsession; she was Ed's. I didn't care about her at all. She was just a means to an end, a way to milk my dick.

As my hips started to thrust and I pulled my full length in and out of her, Ed said, "Be gentle with her, Lincoln."

I jammed myself inside of her harshly, eliciting a cry from her and a glare from Ed. I did not enjoy being told what to do—I'd fuck her how I wanted to fuck her, and Ed would watch and jack off like he always did.

This Stella chick wasn't special, even with her damned eyes. Just another cunt, and she'd end up like all the others.

"Don't tell me how to fuck her," I growled out. Just for that, I'd make sure to be even rougher with her. If she didn't bleed, I'd know I wasn't nearly as rough and wild as I should've been.

When I started to move my hips again, as I savagely dragged myself in and out of her, I watched her chest, watched her breasts bounce with each thrust, her nipples hardened points. She was tight around me, so fucking tight, even though Ed had just been inside of her—and that said nothing about how wet she was. Ed had her good, got her nice and ready for me.

I refused to look at her eyes. I wouldn't do it. I knew other people probably went on and on about her eyes, but I hated them with a passion. It was like her genetics couldn't just pick one like the rest of ours had. No— Stella, the little journalist, had to be *special*.

I realized Stella was busy kissing Ed, even as I pounded into her. No, no that wouldn't work for me.

Once I saw what was happening, I fell on top of her, pushing Ed away. The minute I broke their lip lock, I grabbed her face hard, forcing her head to face the other direction, to stare at the wall, so all she could focus on was the feeling of my prick inside of her, filling her up again and again.

Ed didn't argue. He moved to kneel beside her, running his hand over his dick, which had gotten hard again.

I kept holding her face, refusing to let either of us stare into those damned eyes. If there was a blindfold handy, I would've used it. But holding her head at an awkward and uncomfortable angle was good enough for me. I wanted her to know she was nothing special to either of us. Just a cunt to fuck. Just a pussy to wet our dicks with. Nothing special at all. Something to be used and discarded, like trash.

The first time I came, the orgasm ripped through me, forcing me to arch my back and tense my ass cheeks as my dick spilled inside of her. Knowing she was full of both Ed and mine's cum—the thought always got me hard. Or kept me hard. However you wanted to look at it.

I wasn't done with this woman yet.

I resumed thrusting, going a bit slower now, though I still held her face to the side. Instead of watching her chest bouncing, my eyes drew to Ed, who was lost in himself. One of his hands ran along his dick while the other cupped his balls. Again and again his hand ran over his length, gaining momentum until he ejaculated. I moved, still pounding away at her, watching as his cum shot across her stomach and her breasts. White and sticky.

She looked better covered in his seed. I wondered how she'd look with mine.

So that's what I did: the next time I felt an orgasm building, I pulled out of her and spilled it all on her belly.

Ed and I were like animals, just like we always were when we had someone tied to one of our beds. The hours passed, and eventually we grew tired. Stella had actually fallen asleep, even with her wrists bound and her naked body covered in semen. Spent, worn out, used to the extreme.

I was in the shower, and Ed was at the sink, rubbing shaving cream on his face. Shaving, even though it was two o'clock in the morning. I was no better; my dick was hard again, and I was jacking off as I remembered watching Ed have his way with Stella. She did have a nice, lithe and petite body. I had to give her that. But her eyes? Still hated those fucking things.

It was only because she was tied to the bed and passed out that I asked, "So, when are we going to kill her?" I said it half-jokingly and half serious, because I knew Ed was obsessed with her, but I also knew his obsession wouldn't last. They never did. The longest one had lasted was a month, maybe.

"We're not going to kill her," Ed said, barely blinking an eye at my question. He ran the razor down his cheek slowly.

"We're not?"

"No. I really like her, Lincoln," he went on, cleaning off the razor before doing another line down his face. "You didn't talk to her."

"Sure I did," I said, remembering her acceptance. The way she'd told me to go ahead. There was nothing better than a woman who gave herself up to be used. "I talked to her plenty." The hand pumping my dick started to work harder, and my hips began to thrust as I felt my balls tighten.

Outside of the shower, Ed shook his head. "No, you didn't. You didn't see what I saw at the bar. There's something different about her—" It was literally what he said about all of his preoccupations. "—something off. I think she might be like us, or at least more like us than everyone else. She writes about serial killers, for fuck's sake. If that's not a sign, I don't know what is."

As he spoke, I felt my knees give out a little, and a few shots of cum shot out of my dick, landing in the same place it had the last time I was in the shower. And, just like before, I left it. I'd clean it later.

I turned the water off, flinging open the curtain and glaring at him. "So, by that logic, we should also get newscasters in here, and a lot of the FBI too—"

"That's not what I mean," Ed cut in, throwing me an exasperated look. Well, he wasn't the only one fed up with this conversation. "Have you read any of her articles? They're…just different than anything I've ever read about serial killers before. She's different, Lincoln, I swear it."

I wasn't really sure what I could do with his so-called swearing on it. Stepping out of the shower, I grabbed my towel and muttered, "I give her a week, tops."

Ed's stare turned icy.

"What? You'll get bored, Ed. You will. You always do—not that I'm complaining, because I like what comes after, but her days are numbered, now that she's met us. Don't deny it." I was always a fan of telling the truth, never beating around the bush. Flowery language and meaningless compliments weren't my style.

All Ed said before he finished shaving was, "I'll prove you wrong this time."

I held in a laugh, because I didn't believe him at all.

Stella would die in a week, mark my words.

Chapter Eight - Stella

I must've fallen asleep sometime after Lincoln came. I couldn't remember him leaving, but I did remember him being a grade-A asshole, nowhere near as nice as Ed. I remembered him pushing inside of me with a dick that my vagina practically shook her head at, wordlessly daring the man to get every inch of himself in me. He was thicker and longer, and when he'd been inside, it was both painful and pleasurable.

I suppose I could have been more vehement in telling him no, or even asking him to stop—not that I'd thought he would, either way. From his posture, from the venom laced with his words, I knew Lincoln was not the kind of man who'd listen to someone like me, so it just felt easier to nod and accept whatever he wanted to do to me.

Plus, I was already tied to the bed and worked up. Might as well go all out tonight, right? That's what I had thought at the time, at least.

The men were practically insatiable. I didn't realize men could come so often; I had thought they had limits, or at least had to rest between ejaculations. Their stamina was…amazing. Legendary. There were no other words for it.

And then, sometime during the night, I'd fallen asleep, with my wrists still bound. I'd probably have some bad rugburns in the morning, but I'd deal with them when I got to them. Right now, I was happy in my sex-ridden stupor and dreamless sleep.

In all my life, I'd never dreamt. Or maybe I did, and I just never remembered what the dreams were after waking up. Growing up, I'd heard that was normal. Or Callie would say something along the lines of *I had a crazy dream last night, but now I can't remember it.* My nights could be full of dreams, and I couldn't remember them. But, somehow, I had the feeling I didn't have them at all—because after all, what were the odds I dreamt every night and forgot them all the instant I woke up?

When I compared myself to other people, I always felt weird. Different. My parents had said being different was not necessarily a bad thing, but they had to say things like that; they were parents. It was their job to comfort their child.

Although, after growing up and moving out, comforting me and even being a part of my adult life was not on their to-do list anymore. They hardly spoke to me, hardly talked to me. Never called me. Only when it involved Bree and the upcoming wedding.

I didn't even want to think about the damned wedding.

I turned to my side before I remembered I was tied up, but no ropes held my wrists, and I was able to flip to my side and bury my face in the pillow I was on. It wasn't my pillow, but it still was fluffy and comfy. It smelled like sweat and skin, and I breathed it in deeply, filling my lungs with it. It was a nice smell, even if other women had played a part in making it.

Men like Edward and Lincoln? They probably had new women in their beds every night, since they were so keen on sharing. I mean, Edward had ropes permanently tied to his bedposts, so the writing was already on the wall. I was just reading it.

I was slow to open my eyes, realizing daylight flooded through the windows. I should get home and change. I had to be in the office by noon for a four-hour shift, and I had a blog post to edit before posting. I had to get up.

Sitting, I surveyed the room. I was alone on Edward's bed, my wrists untied and my clothes folded and piled neatly on the nightstand. After scooting to the edge of the bed, I felt something hard and crusty on my stomach and my chest. Couldn't say why it took me so long to remember both men shooting their loads on me, but it did, and when I realized it, I knew I had to shower right away. I couldn't sit in a car for thirty minutes while feeling like this.

So I got up and left the bedroom, still naked, and headed into the bathroom across the hall. I showered using whatever soap was nearest, rinsing off the dried-up cum on my body. It was almost like I was rinsing every bit of Edward and Lincoln away—which made me strangely sad. I didn't want to forget last night.

It was…well, it was fun, even when it was Lincoln inside me, even when he'd grabbed my face and forced me away from Edward. Callie was going to be so jealous once I told her I'd basically had a threesome.

When I was finished, I stepped out and grabbed whatever towel was nearest, drying off my body. I went back into the bedroom and changed into my clothes, checking my cell before sliding it back into my pocket. One message from my mom, who not-so-kindly demanded to know when I had off next week for the damned dress fitting.

My phone was almost dead, so I'd text her back later.

As I meandered downstairs, the smell of bacon and other morning foods wafted to my nose, and I suddenly realized I was *so* hungry. Did I eat dinner last night? I couldn't remember. At the bar, I'd had nuts, half a dozen refills of my pop, and then…a night full of sex. No food.

Huh. Amazing what your body could go through because it was preoccupied with other things.

Edward was in the kitchen, hard at work over the stove, while Lincoln sat on the couch, sprawled out in front of the TV. It was on the early morning news, big red banners on the top and bottom that said *BREAKING NEWS*. I could see his bare shoulders, defined and wide as they were, and I knew he was shirtless.

"Stella, if you have nowhere to be, take a seat. I'm making breakfast. I'll take you back after. You should replenish your body after last night, you're too skinny," Edward rattled off, sounding almost like a parent. It would've been comforting, had Lincoln not chosen that exact moment to throw me a glare.

The second man really did not like me, but that was fine. Most people didn't, once they got to know me. It didn't bother me, and it clearly hadn't bothered him when he was shoving himself between my legs.

I glanced at the clock in the kitchen, finding it was just seven. Still had quite some time before I had to be at work, and if I was honest, I didn't mind spending more time with Edward and his grumpy, pissed-off companion.

Shrugging, I went into the living room, sitting on the couch near Lincoln. The man eyed me all the while, glaring. I did my best to ignore him, but it didn't last long—he was not the type of man to be ignored. Too tall, too thick and muscular, too handsome and too mean.

"I hate your eyes," Lincoln muttered.

At that, I stared squarely at him, waiting for him to explain. In all of my life, I'd never been given that reaction before, and I was curious as to why he was so against them.

Not that I could change them, of course. They were not something about me I could change, unless I wanted colored contacts, in which case the mere thought of sticking something on my eyeballs made me nauseous.

"Lincoln," Edward chimed in from the kitchen, "be nice."

Lincoln, however, would not be nice. He met my stare—my stare which he hated—and said, "It's like I'm staring at two different people, like you're hiding something. I can't tell which one of you is lying."

That was…I didn't know how to respond to him. "I—what makes you think I'm hiding anything?" He thought I hid something just because of my different colored eyes? Heterochromia did not make anyone liars by nature.

"Oh," he said, leaning closer to me. "I'm sure you are. I'm sure you act like a good little girl during the day, but at night you like it rough. You like to be fucked into submission." He grinned, but it was not like the easy smiles Edward had given me. Lincoln's smile was cruel, sadistic, nothing happy about it at all.

It was a smile I kind of liked, in spite of myself.

"You can't play the nice card when I know how naughty you can be," he went on, still leaning closer. It was at that time I realized he only wore athletic shorts, the flimsy kind you got from a sporting goods store—and nothing underneath. His impressive dick was getting hard.

I wondered how in the hell it wasn't sore after last night, because I sure as heck was. Not that I was complaining, because it had been fun in the strangest of ways, but it was like his dick didn't know what a break meant.

I was here as Edward's guest. Surely Lincoln wouldn't just push me down right here and have his way with me while Edward was in the kitchen, slaving away over breakfast? Was it what these guys did? Heat crept up my back at the thought.

What had gotten into me?

"I'm not playing anything," I managed to whisper, turning my head to the floor. Lincoln's face was mere inches from mine, and I didn't quite know what to do. What was acceptable. It wasn't like I was dating Edward or anything, so if something more happened between Lincoln and me, it wouldn't be the end of the world. Plus, after last night, there were hardly any more lines to cross.

"Really?" Lincoln didn't sound impressed or like he believed me. "So if I went underneath those pants, you'd be dry as a bone?"

I nodded, feeling feisty.

"I don't believe you," he whispered, leaning down over me. My back hit the couch's arm, arching me to him. Lincoln placed one hand beside me on the hard couch arm, between me and my escape, and used his other to unbutton my pants like a pro. "I think I'm going to have to teach you a lesson."

As he sluggishly unzipped my jeans, I muttered, "What lesson is that?"

"It's pointless to lie to me," Lincoln said, his lips near my ear, his breath hot on my neck. His hand slipped down, between my underwear and my skin, and I felt him curve along with my body, digging into the pink folds that I knew ached for a certain kind of touch. A kind of touch I had no knowledge of before last night.

My breath caught in my throat, and his lips tickled my neck as his fingers slid along me. Easily, effortlessly, with absolutely no resistance. My entire body responded to his cruel smirk and the cold look in his dark eyes. He looked almost maniacal, and it was an expression I craved.

"Wet," Lincoln whispered, unsurprised. "So wet." As he spoke, he slid a finger inside of me, and I let out a moan. "You liked being used last night, didn't you? Because that's what it was—we used you up, fucked you over and over until you were delirious. Tell me I'm wrong. Tell me you don't want more right now. Tell me this—" He paused as his palm pressed against my clit, the pressure agonizing. "—doesn't make you want more."

"I'm not a liar," I said, glad I was able to at least say something, even though my mind was practically out of my body. He was right. I wanted more. I liked being used. Maybe I wasn't all here, maybe there was a part of me missing, but these guys made me forget all about it.

"Then what do you want?" He wanted to make me say it, and I was about to—had my mouth open and everything, but any words I was about to say caught in my throat when my eyes focused on the TV screen.

More specifically, what was being played on it.

Lincoln did not let my silence discourage him, and he swiftly pulled out his hand from my pants, tugging them down with vigor and eagerness. Just to my knees, just enough so he could access the important part. The part of me that would satisfy his desire.

He worked on yanking down his shorts, popping out his hard length. There was no hesitation in him as he pushed it inside of me. A bit harder to do, given our positions, but like he said, I was almost dripping with wetness. But the TV...

I couldn't tear my eyes off it, even as Lincoln started thrusting, even when Edward yelled from the kitchen, "Be fast, will you? Breakfast is almost done." It didn't even register in my mind his words meant he was more than okay with Lincoln having me whenever he wanted. Clearly, my body wanted it too.

But the goddamn TV, the newscast. The breaking news—it was something I needed to watch, even while being fucked.

The man above me didn't care I wasn't paying attention to him. He just needed one part of me, and it was one part he could have—though I did speak up and say, "Turn up the volume." I swatted his back, causing him to stop pumping me full of his dick and glance around. He grumbled and bitched under his breath, but he reached for the remote and did as I asked.

Huh. So maybe Lincoln wasn't a total jackass after all.

A newscaster woman, all dolled up and far too awake and alert, considering it wasn't even eight yet, was busy describing what police discovered in the late hours of the night the day before, "Local authorities in the Eastland county discovered a body in an abandoned house that was condemned by the city and marked for demolition. Details are slim, but more are arriving as I speak."

An image of a sheriff popped onto the screen, a pre-recorded segment. He was surrounded by reporters who were all clamoring, trying to ask him about it. "I can't share any details with you at this time."

I watched, rapt, nearly forgetting Lincoln was still grunting over me, his dick still hard inside of me. This wouldn't be such news if it was just a body. There was more to this, there had to be.

"Was it an overdose? Another death of the opioid crisis here in America?" one reporter asked, shoving her microphone towards the sheriff.

"It was not an overdose. That's all I can say." And then the sheriff walked off, and the picture cut back to the newswoman.

"That was the sheriff last night," the newswoman said. "But this morning, we learned new information about what is now being called a calculated murder. There are numerous unconfirmed reports of the body being displayed in an almost performative manner. The victim's hands were bound, almost like they were praying."

Lincoln tensed above me, letting out a low groan as he slowly pulled out, his dick wet with my juices and his cum. He put himself away, sitting back as if nothing had happened, like my pants and underwear were not still pulled down. He was not nearly as entranced in the newscast as I was.

I wasn't sure what that said about him, or what it said about me.

I didn't even glance to him as I pulled up my pants. I'd change when I got home, anyways. But this—the topic of the morning news—was so very interesting. A killer who'd displayed his victim was a killer who had thought about it, a crime that was premeditated. A crime of passion never resulted in a victim on display, even if the crime of passion was cleaned up.

No, most criminals, most killers, either left the bodies of their victims or tried to hide them. This was not done by just anyone.

The way it was a media frenzy, the way the newscaster spoke about it, I knew there was more to it she wasn't sharing. Had the killer done something else to the body? How did he keep the body erect? Dead bodies didn't just sit on their own accord. What I would give to be a fly on the wall of that house.

My mind was swimming, even as Edward gave me a plate of hefty breakfast, eggs and bacon and sausage. A glass of orange juice, too. All I could think about was the body, the way the sheriff had looked pale, almost like he'd seen something horrible. There had to be more to it. There was something they weren't saying, something they weren't allowed to say, otherwise it might cause a county-wide panic.

Did Easton county have its own serial killer in the making?

Chapter Nine - Stella

I had Edward drop me back off at the bar, knowing it probably wasn't good to let a stranger—even though I'd slept with both him and his roommate more than once—know where I live. It was on my walk home that my phone rang, and I picked it up, seeing it was Callie.

"Where the hell are you?" Callie practically screamed on the other line. "Are you okay? I've been texting you left and right, girl. Have you seen the news? Of course you have. You probably knew about it the second it happened, with your sick sense for serial killers—"

Didn't even get a hello, not that I expected one.

"I don't have a sense about them, I just find them interesting. And yes, I did see the news. I'm heading home real fast to change, and then I'm going to work early. I know there's probably enough coverage about it, but if anyone gets to write about it, it's me," I said.

"You're one crazy bitch, but you know I love you. Now, I'm going to ask again, because you didn't answer me: where are you? Did you not come home last night?" There was a pause on the other end as Callie inhaled a great, giant gasp. "Tell me you didn't go home with Killian. Tell me you didn't fuck your boss!" Based on her tone, she wanted me to admit I did.

"No, Killian had some other company last night," I said, thinking about him and Sandy in the women's restroom at the bar. "I, uh…I might've gone home with someone I met at the bar."

Callie was silent for a while. "Holy shit. I need stories. I'm home now, but I got to run. Tonight. You better tell me some juicy details tonight."

I laughed and said, "I will." After hanging up, I walked through the streets of our town, heading through the commercial district. The bar wasn't too far of a walk from my house, but with morning rush hour traffic, it took longer to cross the roads and wait for red lights.

By the time I got to our house, Callie was already gone. I came in through the front door, locking it behind me. I hurriedly changed and grabbed my bag, my trusted laptop and a few notebooks inside. My phone was nearly dead, so I grabbed the charger. Hopefully I could get a seat at the coffee shop near an outlet, so I could charge it while I wrote.

Because there was a lot to write about, even without seeing the scene.

Within the hour, I was at the Tribune's office, pushing through its front door with gusto. I was almost smiling, *almost*. My presence stunned my coworkers— the ones who were there, anyway. Some of them weren't at work, presumably because of their hangovers. The booze had been flowing last night like a waterfall.

I kept my bag around my shoulders, fiddling with the strap as I walked through the cluttered space. In the far back, I saw Killian sitting in his office, nursing a coffee and rubbing his forehead. Oh, I bet he had a killer migraine. A dark part of me hoped it hurt.

I knocked once on the glass encasing his office before walking in and sitting in the chair facing him.

He practically leapt up, nearly spilling his coffee mug all over his desk. Luckily he only jerked it a little, but his full attention was on me, weirdly enough. "Stella," he said, "I was worried about you. Last night, you just left. You didn't tell anyone goodbye, so I thought…"

He thought what? Something bad had happened to me? Something bad *did* happen—though it wasn't strictly bad as it was rather naughty. Either way, he didn't need to know all the details.

I let the silence linger for a while. "You thought what?"

"Well," Killian said, rubbing the back of his neck in a nervous gesture, "I saw you talking to a guy at the bar, and I thought…" Still, he couldn't say it.

"You thought *what*?" I prodded again, this time putting emphasis on the final word.

"I thought I saw you leaving with him." He squeezed his eyes shut as he drank some of his coffee. "Everything's a little fuzzy. I had a bit too much to drink—"

"I'm sure not everything is fuzzy." I wasn't sure why I said it. I didn't have any reason to be jealous of what Killian and Sandy did—the latter who wasn't here yet, I'd noticed. It was something I shouldn't have said, because he would undoubtedly think I was jealous.

Maybe I had been, last night as I listened to the starting sounds of a blowjob. But after everything that happened last night, and technically this morning, I wasn't.

Or I shouldn't be.

"What…" Killian trailed off the moment his green eyes met mine. Recognition flashed in their depths, and he was quick to turn a certain shade of pink I bet he turned last night, when Sandy's mouth was around his dick. He knew I knew, and it's why he said, "Stella, I—"

Again, I cut him off, "It doesn't matter." His excuses were unnecessary. "I didn't come here to talk about who you're with." It was a good sidetrack to take so he wouldn't bring up Edward again.

It was a while before Killian glanced at his computer. "You don't start work for another few hours. Why are you here so early?" He was just now realizing it. My boss was not the sharpest tool in the shed.

"I want to write about the body they found."

He blinked, letting my words sink in. "You—they found a body? Where?"

"Did you not hear the news?" My heart thumped in my chest, so loud and hard it threatened to break out. How in the world could he not have heard the news?

Killian held up a finger, leaned to his keyboard, and started typing something in. His eyes scanned the screen, and I watched as sweat pooled on his brow. His eyes were bloodshot, and he looked tired. Did Sandy keep him up all night?

"That's…fifteen minutes from here," he slowly said, glancing to me after he was done, watching as I took in the news. Fifteen minutes from here? So we had an address… "What more could you write about? The news is all over it."

"My articles are mostly speculation. Plus, readers will expect me to write about it. If my articles were already the most visited on our website, imagine the traffic once I start writing about this."

"You're assuming this incident isn't going to be isolated. You're expecting more."

I nodded. "I am, and not just because I'm obsessed with killers."

Killian flinched at my words. "Look, if this is about what I said last night, I'm sorry. I shouldn't have said it. It was rude and uncalled for, and I didn't mean it." He seemed genuine with his words today, but he was stupid if he thought this was about last night.

"This has nothing to do with last night," I swore. "Nothing at all. I'm going to write about this, Killian, whether or not you give me your go ahead. I think it would be good for the Tribune."

He sighed. "What are you going to do? How many articles are you going to write about this?"

"Depends on how things go from here," I answered honestly. "And I want to go to the house."

"It's still probably a crime scene."

"Then they'll let me walk around the yellow tape."

Killian let out a groan, and he rubbed his neck again. More than a nervous tick—it was something he did when he was anxious. It was kind of cute. "Fine, but anytime you're investigating for these articles, I'm coming with you, do you understand? This isn't something you can mess around with."

Did he not know me at all? I was not the type of person to *mess around* no matter what I was doing, especially when it came to my articles.

I realized he was waiting for me to agree, so I begrudgingly said, "Fine." And then, it was the weirdest thing—I noted the concern in his gaze and couldn't help but wonder if he was worried about me. My safety. My life.

Seemed a silly thing to worry about when life was so fleeting.

Before I let him completely relax, I added, "I want to go now."

Killian let out another long sigh, not surprised by my sudden need to go to the crime scene. "Fine. Let me put this in a travel mug, first."

Once the manly diva was ready, we got in his car and left. He put the address into his GPS and, like he said, it was less than a fifteen-minute drive from the Tribune's offices, on the other side of town from my house. The police were still in the area, combing the house and the yard for clues. Killian parked his car along the curb down the street, and as he got out and spoke to the police about who we were and why we were here, I slowly got out of the car and studied the houses around us.

This was perhaps the oldest part of town. The houses here had been built decades ago, before this town had its own department and grocery stores. Seventy years old or more, most of them were run down. Siding chipped and front porches rotted. None of them were as bad as the house that was the crime scene though—the house where the body was found was beyond decrepit, zoning papers taped to the front door, useless as they were.

And I meant decrepit in the worst sense: windows broken, front door hanging off its hinges. Looked like its foundation was cracked and falling apart. A gravel driveway covered in weeds and dead grass. The house's roof was in shambles, some of the shingles hanging off the side of the two-story house.

It looked like shit. No wonder the city condemned this address. No bank could ever sell a house like this, even to flippers. This was beyond repair. Best tear it down and start anew.

With my messenger bag over my shoulder, I met Killian on the sidewalk. Killian was busy putting away his wallet, holding his coffee in his other hand. "They said we could look around, but not to touch anything," he said. "And obviously don't cross the yellow tape."

I took the lead, moving closer to the house, creeping around its side, hugging the yellow caution tape as I went. Killian was glued to my back, and I pretended not to feel his eyes watching me. The man never knew when to take a chill pill.

"The body was found in the basement," he said.

"The basement?" I echoed, glancing at him. That didn't sound right.

"He said forensics is going to be here a while, because it was…messy."

My feet stopped as I stared at a broken square window on the house's lower wall, the window to the basement. If it was messy, it meant there had to be blood, right? I wanted to see it.

"The basement leaks like a bitch, so they have to get all the evidence they can before the next storm."

"Which is…"

Killian answered, "In the next few days, I think."

I filed this away in my head. I'd never before thought about trespassing on a crime scene, but I might have to do it, once the cops were out of here.

This neighborhood…it wasn't the kind of neighborhood where everyone sat outside and had cookouts and talked to each other. This street was the kind of street where you only paid attention to yourself.

When Killian gagged behind me, I stopped, breathing in deeply through my nose. The air was rank in the space between the condemned house and its neighbor, nearest where the basement window was. It was the worst stench I'd ever smelled in my life. Rotten and putrid. I wanted to throw up.

Holding a hand over my nose and my mouth, I knew all I needed to to write my first article about it. I moved past Killian, and he all too willingly followed me back to the sidewalk, where the air was clear.

"That's it?" he asked, surprised. "We came here for a *drive-by*?"

"We got out," I said, heading back to the car. I was the first one inside.

What did Killian expect? For me to whip out a magnifying glass and play the detective? No, I didn't need to spend any more time here. I knew enough. I knew more than enough. The only thing I did not know was the victim's identifying information.

"Do we know who the victim was? Male, female? Old, young?" I asked him as he got in the car.

"The cop referenced the victim as a she, so…female, but as for an age, I didn't think to ask, since this is your story and not mine," Killian remarked dryly as he set his coffee in the cup holder and drove off. His green eyes flicked to me. "You didn't even take any notes."

"I didn't need to."

Killian sighed—he did that a lot when he was around me. I must drive him crazy. "I need more coffee."

"I know just the place," I said, nodding along, knowing he wanted Starbucks, like the majority of other people did. Why have that when you could go to a cozy, homey, small town coffee shop whose prices were less than half?

With any luck, Killian wouldn't stay. He'd get his coffee and go, leave me to draft my next article in peace. After seeing the house, I had a lot of thoughts, and all of them revolved around the possibility there was a killer out there just starting to learn his craft.

Chapter Ten - Edward

I worked as a chef at a high scale restaurant that was a good forty-minute drive from our house. Most of my workday was spent alone, though the other chefs always tried to talk to me. I laughed and smiled when necessary, but I didn't really want to talk to them. Sometimes talking to people was nothing but a chore.

Lincoln always said I was the most normal out of the two of us, but I had my days. Yes, some days I wanted to strangle every single person I met, regardless of whether or not they spoke to me or even looked at me. The world was too full as it was; I'd be doing it a favor.

And then there were days like today, when my mind was so wrapped up in someone else that I couldn't seem to get any of my dishes right. Too salty, too much cayenne. Overcooked, undercooked. Raw. My mind was so lost in thinking about last night my work suffered, and food—food was one good thing about life. I couldn't mess up anyone's meals. My pride wouldn't let me. Meaning I had to re-cook over a dozen meals before twelve rolled around, but it was what it was.

No matter how much I tried to not let Stella dominate my mind, I failed, so eventually I just gave in. I thought about her a lot as the day wore on and the hours passed me by. Work never dragged for me, because I sincerely enjoyed what I did, but today—today I wanted nothing more than to leave and go to Stella, wherever she was. I knew where she worked, because I did my fair share of stalking, but I didn't know where she lived.

That would have to change soon.

It made sense she had a roommate; Stella did not seem like the kind of woman who'd do well living alone. There was something about her that was…indescribable. Something hidden beneath the surface, something begging me to find out more about her.

I was drawn to her in the strangest of ways, the most natural of ways. I wanted her more than I'd ever wanted anyone before—and that was saying something. Lincoln always said I obsess over things, and I suppose he was right to an extent, but I would swear up and down my feelings for Stella were unlike anything I'd ever felt before. I had to know more about her.

I had to see her again, had to have her tied to my bed again. This time, I'd take her pale, thin ankles and tie them so tightly she'd leave with rope burns. I wanted to taste her—to make her wriggle and writhe and scream my name.

Fuck. I was getting aroused just thinking about what I would do to her, what I craved doing to her. Work was not a good place to have an erection.

If I could've stopped it I would have, but I couldn't, so I spent the next few minutes hugging myself to the counter, where I worked on slicing through chicken. The aroma of the kitchen was not enough to take me out of my mind, and I was too weak to fight the thoughts of Stella swarming through me.

Weak.

That was funny, because I was anything but weak. I was strong, physically and mentally, and I knew what I wanted in life. There were only a select few things I enjoyed, and I knew Lincoln felt the same—in that respect, we weren't normal. However try as anyone might, if someone ever looked into our lives and our, let's call them, *hobbies*, they would find no evidence of what we'd done. No evidence at all.

One of the pluses of being a cop, Lincoln assured me, along with coming from a family who dealt with that sort of thing for a living. He knew how to deal with the bodies, knew how to clean up the blood quickest. He had a system, and he refused to tell me what that system was, as a failsafe. If something ever were to happen, and somehow the clues led back to him, I would not get dragged under with him. I would still be free.

I was thankful to him for doing it, for finding me and showing me how to live this life without drawing everyone's attention. Years ago, when I was nothing more than a weird kid of thirteen, I was just starting to dabble in the deaths of animals. More specifically, my neighbor's dog. That damned thing never stopped barking, and if I was honest, it was my first victim because I knew its silence would make the neighborhood happy.

Get to sate my urge to kill and quiet the neighborhood. What wasn't good about it?

Of course, it was after the neighbor's third missing dog that they started looking at me. The neighbors had stormed around the fence separating our yards and noticed recently-dug dirt. My parents were not the type of people who cared what I did, and the lawn was my responsibility, so it was the perfect hiding place...or so my little thirteen-year-old mind had thought.

When my parents found out what I did, when the neighbors forced them to make me dig up their dead dogs, they weren't happy. What normal parents would be thrilled at the prospect of their only son catching and mutilating the neighbor's dogs?

It wasn't long before my parents tried to have me committed, put into a hospital to be watched. I'd heard them talking, and I decided enough was enough. If they didn't want me around, I wouldn't stay. So I left. I packed a single bag and left through my bedroom window before anyone could come to take me away, before my parents could pack me into the car and drive me there. Whatever.

I was homeless for a while, begging on the streets, avoiding any location where I knew my parents might frequent. I grew my hair out, and with the dirt and grease of being homeless—and therefore shower-less—I looked far different.

It was a dark night when I first saw Lincoln. I had been asleep in an alleyway, off the streets, near another homeless man. Carl, I called him, though I was never sure if it was actually his name or not. He was missing too many teeth to understand his speech.

Lincoln was a few years older than me, but I had known that first moment what he was, what he pretended to be. He was just like me, even as he pointed to the sleeping homeless man beside me. I peeked through slit eyelids, watching as another man nodded and grabbed the homeless man, saying something about giving Carl a warm meal for free. To lure him to a second location.

Turned out, the secondary location was an abandoned warehouse that had been commandeered to suit another purpose. I followed them—it wasn't too hard, considering their fancy black BMW stuck out like a sore thumb in the area of town we were in. I knew instantly Lincoln came from money, but it wasn't until I hunched in the darkness, in the shadows of the warehouse and watched the scene unfold I knew where their money came from.

Death.

The homeless man's mouth was gagged, and he was tied to a support beam. He tried to struggle, but it was pointless. The older man had talked to Lincoln as if instructing him, as if teaching him what to do.

As I listened, I realized death was not always bloody. Death did not always involve dismemberment. Death could be accidental; it could be as simple as falling down stairs or stepping out in front of a car. I learned then when Lincoln's family was involved, death tended to happen more often.

I still liked to call them assassins, but Lincoln and his family were always vehement against the term. Too flashy, and far too illegal.

The homeless man they'd taken—my buddy Carl—was being used as instruction: where the vital organs were in a malnourished body, where to cut to have him bleed out within minutes. It was before the homeless man met his demise that Lincoln turned his head and stared straight at the shadows I crouched in. He'd known I was there the whole time.

Instead of killing me, like I thought they were going to do as the older man dragged me out and threw me on the ground before Lincoln and the restrained homeless man, Lincoln studied me, tapping the knife he held against his palm.

And then he'd given the knife to me, saying not a word.

It was all history from there, mostly bloody history. I was grateful to Lincoln and his family for taking me in, even more grateful to them for showing me how to satisfy my urges while being careful, while knowing what to do to not get caught. They didn't often let me take marks—which was what they called their targets—because my methods were always a bit too bloody, but they let me hunt and use their resources when I needed to.

Because that's what it was: a need. An urge, a desire. I needed to kill to live, as much of an oxymoron as it was. I needed to watch someone breathe their last breath as I lived on, had to be the one to make the final blow. The rush of power that came with ending someone's life was a beauty most people would never know, because they were too caught up in following society's strict moral rules.

Being unrestricted and unrestrained when it came to morals felt so good, I was surprised more people didn't try it.

Well, some did, and they were immediately caught. I did not like to think about those people, because I thought myself better than them, I thought myself on a whole different level entirely.

It was on my first break that I went into the back room and pulled out my cell phone after washing my hands. I knew I shouldn't call her, but I had to hear Stella's voice. I had to feel close to her, even though there were cities between us. So I called her.

She didn't pick up on the first ring. She probably stared at the caller ID, her eyebrows slightly together, a confused look on her face. Stella probably wondered just what the hell my name was doing flashing across her screen. I hadn't outright given her my number.

Stella was slow to pick up, answering tentatively, "Edward?"

Oh, the timbre of her voice could soothe me eternally. Her voice could call me back from the edge of insanity. I didn't know much about this woman, but I swore to myself that would change. I would discover everything about her, and it still wouldn't be enough.

"It's me," I spoke with a smile, as if she could see it. Stella herself hardly smiled, but I knew she was capable of it. She was just…so different from anyone I'd ever met. "How are you?"

Stella didn't answer me right away; instead she asked, "How did you get my number? And why are you in my phone? I don't remember…"

My eyes flicked around the break room. I was in here alone, and the door was shut, so I spoke honestly, "While you were naked and passed out in my bed, I found your phone. I knew I'd have to have more of you, Stella."

Did she enjoy the sound of my voice like I did hers? I had an awful thought then. What if she didn't want to see me again? What if last night was just one night? I couldn't afford to think like that. Not yet.

"Edward," she said my name again, and it was all I needed to hear. She wasn't mad.

Candace Wondrak

"What are you doing?"

"I'm planning an article." Her answer was simple and honest, and I knew the article was about what was on the news earlier. She had been so rapt in the newscast she hardly even blinked when Lincoln shoved his dick inside of her.

"Another one about serial killers?" If only she knew who she talked to, if only she knew what I was—there would be no hesitation from her then.

"Yes," she whispered.

I heard the sounds of bells ringing, and I waited a moment before asking, "Where are you?" I had to picture her, had to imagine where she was, though it was hard to do any of it when I couldn't get the image of her, naked and restrained on my bed out of my head.

"I'm at a coffee shop. It's where I do most of my writing," she said.

I pictured her sitting alone at a table, a laptop or a tablet open in front of her, a focused look on her pretty face. Those eyes—those wondrously strange eyes—flicking back and forth as they reread and checked over what she'd written so far.

Lincoln didn't like her eyes, but I did. I loved them.

"I need to see you again," I said, my urgency plain. The truth was I needed to see her now, but that was impossible for a number of reasons, distance aside. I couldn't just walk out of my job anytime I wanted.

It was a minute before she asked, "When?" Stella didn't ask why, because she knew. Only an oblivious fool wouldn't know why I needed to see her.

If I said tonight, would she think me needy? Would it be too soon? I didn't want to scare her off. Though I needed her right this instant, I said, "Tomorrow night."

Not as a question but as a statement. Stella couldn't deny me my release even if she wanted to.

And she didn't.

I really wanted to know where she lived, but I didn't push when she said, "I'll meet you at the bar at seven." And then she hung up, not one for small talk, apparently. But I didn't mind. I had a location and a time, and I couldn't wait to see her, let alone do more digging about her online tonight.

The day could not pass quickly enough.

Chapter Eleven - Killian

When I came back with two coffees, I found Stella putting away her phone. I'd pretended not to listen as I was in line waiting, but it was hard not to, because this place was small and the opposite of crowded and noisy. It was a quaint, quiet place, and I could understand why she liked coming here to write her articles.

Plus, it wasn't too far from the Tribune, so when she pushed her deadlines—something she did more often than not—she didn't have to run too far, since she didn't have a car.

Partly my fault, I supposed. I couldn't hire her as a full-time journalist because hiring was not my decision. I didn't own the paper, but I had to listen to its owners when it came to staffing and assigning hours.

The owners hadn't even wanted me to hire Stella to begin with. That had been a fight, but it was one I would gladly do again. I'd known from the first moment I met her that she was special. And no, not only because of her unique, alluring gaze.

Even when I was with Julie, I had known Stella was special, that there was more to her than most people saw. I didn't think myself a haughty person, but I didn't think I was like the next average Joe, either.

I really wished I wouldn't have gotten drunk and came on to her at the Christmas party last year, and I'd give anything to take back what I said last night.

Alcohol always affected me it seemed, and I was not a nice person under its influence. I should probably stop drinking altogether, and really try my hardest with Stella.

Because, even while drunk, even after walking away from her and almost getting a blowjob from another woman, she still would not leave my head.

I set her coffee down beside her laptop, sitting in the chair across from her. In spite of myself, in spite of trying to act calm and collected, I asked, "Who was that?" I watched her take a leisurely sip of her coffee—black, sugarless, and utterly disgusting. I didn't know how she could drink it like that.

"My mom wants to know when I have off next week so I can get measured for my maid of honor dress," Stella said, her eyes focusing on me. I noticed how she didn't exactly answer my question, but if she wanted to hide things from me, I couldn't blame her. She had every right not to trust me with certain details of her life, because I was just her boss.

Just her damned boss.

God, I really wished I could change that. I didn't want to be just her boss. I wanted more. I'd wanted more from her ever since meeting her, even when I was with Julie. Never would I admit it aloud, unless it was in confidence—something I didn't have from Stella, after the way I'd acted toward her.

I was a fucking douchebag.

"Take off whenever you need," I said, oozing generosity I would never show to anyone else. "I'll let you make up the hours." Stupid, because I never let anyone make up their time, but for Stella, I was willing to break every rule.

"Thank you. I'll tell her and then let you know what day I won't be in."

After taking another sip from the cup, Stella's fingers started to type furiously on her keyboard, and I watched for a while in silence, amazed at how different she looked while she was concentrating on something.

Who the hell was I to try to stop her from writing about what she liked to write about? I gave her the go-ahead to write about what she wanted, and it just so happened she liked to write about killers. Serial killers. A bit weird, not normal by any means, but a hobby was a hobby. She was knowledgeable about them—and her online articles were our most-visited on the website, it was true.

"So what did our little jaunt to the crime scene do?" I asked, curious. We hadn't been there for long, and I wasn't sure what the hell she might've gleaned from it. Was she that good? Just a quick peek around and she knew? Or at least *thought* she knew?

Because, the truth was, no one really could know. No one knew what went on inside someone's head. Sometimes a person didn't even know what went on inside his own head. Cogs turned, wheels moved; sometimes a person was so lost in his or her own delusions they couldn't see what was real and what wasn't.

Minds were…fascinating things.

Maybe that's why I liked Stella so much—I knew her mind was hiding something. I knew just from looking at her there was a part of her she hid from the world. It would probably never happen, but I wanted to be the catalyst, the spark that released whatever it was.

I wanted her.

"It told me a lot, actually," she said, glancing to me. No matter how many times she stared at me with those eyes, I could never get over how different they were from each other. Normally heterochromia was a slight difference, wasn't it? How many other people out there had a bright blue eye along with a warm brown one? No hints of green anywhere, no brown diluting her blue.

I knew Stella hated it when people commented on her eyes, when they acted like she was different just because her eyes were unique. I'd heard her complain about it before, which was why I never spoke a compliment to her about it aloud, and I did my best not to linger on one eye too long.

That damned blue one was always calling my attention, though. It was hard to ignore its sapphire depth.

"Told you what?" I asked, flicking my gaze around the shop. There was only one other person here, a man fiddling on his phone in the corner. He was here before we got here, and it looked like the man would be here long after we left. How someone could spend their free time in a coffee shop and actually enjoy their life, I'd never know.

A small tweak of a smile graced Stella's lips, but only for a moment. "You'll have to wait and read the article like everyone else." She was…almost teasing me. Her somewhat petulant tone made me grin.

Always surprising me, this one. I think I loved her, all of my stupid decisions aside.

When silence overtook us, when I could hear nothing but the tapping of her fingers against the keyboard, I straightened my back. I knew I couldn't stay here much longer—anytime I was away during work hours, something always seemed to go wrong at the Tribune. Honestly, it wouldn't surprise me if the entire building caught on fire or something.

But I couldn't leave yet. Not before clearing the air.

"Stella," I said, waiting until her fingers slowed and she rose her stare to me. "I really am sorry about what I said last night. I shouldn't have said it. You didn't deserve that. It was a dick move."

She nodded, saying nothing. She had to agree with everything I said, otherwise surely she would've said something.

"And as for the whole thing with Sandy—"

That she had to comment on. "I don't care who you're with, Killian." Her lips thinned, a pensive look crossing her face. "But Sandy? She's...nice enough, I guess, but for you? You deserve someone better."

Damn right I deserved someone better. I deserved someone like Stella. Before getting drunk and letting Sandy drag me into the woman's restroom, I hadn't had any woman's mouth on any part of me for months. Ever since finally breaking up with Julie. Horrible as some might think it, I had been celibate since the breakup. With any luck, my perseverance would pay off.

Because I wanted Stella.

I loved Stella.

She was right, of course. I should never have let Sandy take my hand, and I definitely should've stopped her long before she went down on me. I was drunk and weak, and I'd never let alcohol get the better of me again.

"I mean, I like Sandy, but..." Stella shrugged. "She can be mean sometimes. I don't know if it's because of her divorce or what, but she always finds a way to make fun of me." She rubbed her arms, looking too thin across from me. She must've only weighed a hundred or so pounds.

Far too skinny. She needed more meat on those bones.

Her words struck a chord with me. Sandy was mean to her? I hadn't noticed any of that, but maybe it's because I was so busy in the office, and Sandy and Stella's work hours rarely crossed. If what Stella said was true, and I didn't doubt her a bit, then Sandy and I needed to have a talk. There would be no workplace bickering, especially when it came to Stella.

Stella was a woman, but with the way she looked, how small she was in both height and weight, she was like a girl. Helpless in a way. I wanted to protect her from the world, even though I knew she would swear up and down she needed no protection, needed no help. But it was something everyone learned eventually: even the best of us needed help sometimes. She was no exception.

"I know I'm the last person who should ask you this, but…" God, I sounded like a dweeb. Like someone who'd never asked someone out before. I trailed off, unsure. Maybe I shouldn't. Maybe I should wait.

But then again, maybe if I waited, one of us would be dead in a week. You never knew. Things happened.

"But what?" Stella prodded.

"I'd like to see you," I broke my silence, meeting her questioning eyes. "Outside of work, I mean. I want to take you to dinner." Cringy, even to my ears. I couldn't imagine how bad I sounded to hers.

She tilted her head, some of her brown hair falling in her face. Today she wore it down, not up in her usual messy bun. Blinking, she slowly said, "Are you asking me out? Is a boss even supposed to ask out one of his employees?"

"That depends. Are you going to come after me with a lawsuit? I warn you now, I might look well-dressed, but I don't have much in my bank account."

Again, a tiny smile. I lived for those fucking things.

"I have stuff to write, I don't have time for lawsuits," Stella said. "But…maybe I'd have time for a date with you. When?"

Okay, this was when I should just let it go, but I couldn't. I wasn't the type to just let things go. My parents hadn't raised me like that. So I said, "What about tomorrow at seven?" As I said it, I watched her reaction, waiting for her to confess that she'd made, what sounded like, another date tomorrow with someone.

That stranger at the bar I thought I'd saw her leave with?

No. I wouldn't think about it.

"I can't tomorrow. What about Friday?" She offered the suggestion so easily, it was hard for me to feel slighted at the missed opportunity of tomorrow.

"You work Friday, right?" A stupid question, because I knew she worked. I made the damn schedule. "We can go right after work, unless you'd like to go home and change?" I knew where she lived, but I'd never been there. Seemed a huge line to cross, and once it was crossed, there was no going back, no more pretending.

Us humans were good at pretending.

"Friday after work," Stella said, reaffirming me.

I was so happy to have a date with Stella, so full of possibilities I neglected to realize the man in the corner of the shop staring at us.

Or, more specifically, at *her*.

Chapter Twelve - Stella

The dress fitting was on Tuesday. I couldn't forget, so I made a note on the fridge the next day. As I was writing it down, Callie emerged from the hall, wearing a business suit and heels that clicked on the tile. Her brown, highlighted hair was straightened, little wisps of it framing her face. Her dark brown eyes were framed with smoky eyeshadow, blush on her cheeks. With her clothes hugging her curves, she looked good. Sexy and professional at the same time.

"So," Callie said, grabbing her purse, "excited for your date tonight with the hotties?"

I'd told her all about what had happened with Edward and Lincoln—and she'd been extremely jealous. Two men at once was her dream, she'd joked. All she'd ever had was one guy and another woman before.

This was before John, though. Now she was strictly monogamous.

"Well, I made it with Edward, so I don't know if I'll see Lincoln tonight." As I said it, I secretly hoped I'd see both. They were two different men, and they filled different parts of me. Who knew I liked it rough? Who knew I liked a man who wasn't afraid to take what he wanted?

When Killian had tried to make his moves on me last year, he'd been drunk. I was never a fan of drunks.

They smelled, and their behavior was sorely lacking, usually. Killian had been no different.

I hoped our date tomorrow would go differently. Hell, I still wasn't sure why I'd said yes to him.

"Oh, with how you described them? I bet they never have their women one on one. Always sharing. Super jealous right now, which you already know." Callie waited a moment before adding, "And a date with Killian tomorrow. You're getting more action than me, Stella! I won't be able to see John for a few days. He's out of town on some business trip." She made an annoyed noise.

More action. I didn't exactly want loads of action, but I couldn't deny the fact it did seem like I was going to be tripping over penises in the next two days. Granted, it wasn't like I planned on sleeping with Killian—Edward and Lincoln though? I would be a liar if I said I wasn't expecting to be with them, or at least Edward.

So weird, because a few days ago, I was a virgin in every sense of the word. Now it was like my inner slut emerged, and she felt good hanging out and getting some. Who was I to deny my body the basic pleasure of life—meaning sex?

"My date with Killian is just a date," I said, moving to lean on the island opposite her. "And I don't have high hopes for it, after everything that happened with him in the past."

"You know it could end badly, right? He could try to get some from you again, and you deny him, and then—bam! You're fired. I know you love your job at the Tribune," Callie explained, "and I don't want to see you hurt." She moved around the counter, enveloping me in a hug. "I hope you know what you're doing…" The hug ended, and she smiled as she released me. "And being careful. You are still on the pill, right? Taking it at the same time each day?"

I rolled my eyes. "Yes, *Mom*."

She laughed, grabbed her purse, and was out the door in less than a minute.

I spent my day fixing up my next blog post and working on my article. I had to go into the office for a few hours to do my time, as they say, but within four hours I was home and showering. My date with Edward and hopefully Lincoln drew near, and I wanted every inch of me clean.

Would they tie me up again? Would they do something else to me, something more? Or would they not have as much interest in me, since they already had me? They didn't seem like the type of guys who stuck with one woman for long, and I supposed I couldn't blame them. Men were always so cavalier about sex and relationships, because they weren't the ones who could get pregnant.

I wouldn't let my pessimism downplay what I felt toward them. Feelings I couldn't explain. I was, shockingly enough, *excited* to see them again. I *wanted* to see them, to spend more time with them. I wanted them to fuck me.

Just…whoa. What crazy alien took command of my brain when I wasn't looking? I never had thoughts like those, never ever wanted any guy—let alone more than one—to fuck me. I wasn't acting like myself.

And I felt great. I felt happy.

I dressed in leggings and a longer shirt, even did my makeup a little bit. Something I never did, because it just seemed pointless to me, something that would inevitably smear or wash off, but I wanted to look nice. I wanted, I realized, to impress Edward and Lincoln. I wanted them to want me more than once.

A drug.

What I sought to be for them was a drug. I wanted them addicted to me, similar to how I had grown addicted to them after a single night. The tables should turn on them, it was only fair. They should crave me as much as I craved them, and if they didn't want me by the end of the night, then maybe it wasn't meant to be.

After being with them, I knew.

I just knew I had to be with someone who knew they needed me. Someone who could show it through their actions, because when it came to words...well, words were often lies. At least when they were spoken to me. Actions didn't lie.

I didn't view myself as someone who needed to have a boyfriend to survive. I'd lived this long alone and could keep going. But the thing was, I didn't *want* to. Not anymore. Not after being with Edward and Lincoln.

Those guys had made me addicted to them after a single night. If I did not become the drug they needed to survive...I didn't know what I would do. Something not pretty, probably.

After I was ready for my date, I noticed I still had some time, so I sat down and pulled out my laptop, rereading my article. It wasn't due until tomorrow at the end of the workday for Sunday's paper, but for once it would be nice to not have to rush to email it to Killian for review.

It was...perfect.

Dear reader, you know I come to you and tell you only truths. I would never lie to you, while other media would see fit to keep shoving lies and mismanaged newscasts down your throat. By now, you've undoubtedly heard about the body.

Yes, the body.

I don't need to describe what body or where it was found, because if you're reading this, you already know. By the time this article hits the shelves and the website, you'll have already heard all about it on the TV, the radio, the chitchat you and your coworkers partake in every morning before getting to work.

You already know there was a body found in a condemned house on one of the oldest streets in our town. By now, you've heard it was a young woman, her identity still not released to the public yet, in respect for the family. Maybe that will change by the time this goes to press. But I digress.

You, reader, might think I'm here to talk about what happened to her, and in a way, you'd be right. But in another way, you're wrong. What interests me is not the victim but the perpetrator. Who would ever murder a young woman in the basement of an abandoned, foreclosed house and restrain her hands so it looked like she was praying?

A killer, obviously.

All right, so we might have a new killer in town, to which you might be thinking: that's not bad. There's a killer in every town. The murder rates in

Chicago are much higher than in our state. We'll be okay.

I write this to ask you—no, to tell you—this is only the beginning. This was the first, but I promise you it won't be the last body the police find. How do I know this? Deduction.

The woman was brought to the house from another location, which suggests some degree of premeditation. Not that I'm suggesting any killer is an average, everyday, run-of-the-mill killer, but I don't think anyone's first thought after murdering someone would be to display the body.

I'm going to take a pause here and let you think on this yourself. If someone planned out a murder, if someone wanted the body on display and moved the victim into a praying position, what does that mean? The cops would tell you it was just some sick individual who needs some cold-hearted justice, but I would tell you it's because our killer had the hopes of someone finding the victim.

You don't put something on display if you don't want other people to look at it. We're very curious by nature, us humans. This victim, the poor girl, was no different from a trophy...

...but she wasn't a trophy, and that isn't all of the puzzle.

Why would our killer choose an abandoned house, a property no one is supposed to go onto, to display his crime? Why would he leave her there to rot? He chose the location for privacy, and I was there—the air still smelled like flies and rotting skin, one of the worst smells I'd ever had the displeasure of breathing in—but to display his victim in the basement and leave her there, it suggests to me something else.

Our killer was testing the waters. This was not his finale or even his grand opening. This was his practice test, his dry run. This was the instrumentalist playing his violin on a stage before no people.

Long story short, I think our killer is only getting started. I think this is just the beginning of the bloody mayhem he'll bring us. The next time he kills, he'll get better. Better and better until he thinks he's good enough to reveal his victims to the public.

Make no mistake, the only reason the police discovered this body was because the smell was so strong, you could smell it even while not on the property. The smell was the only reason the police were called to investigate, because the houses next door are still occupied. Who wants to breathe in and smell the stink and decay of human flesh? Not me, and I hope not you.

Of course, this means our killer could be active out there, somewhere. He might've already killed again, but until there are more crimes committed, until there are more victims piling up in a similar way, he remains only a killer. I would put all the money I have—which isn't much, sadly for me—on him killing again, and doing it soon. I would bet my life that by the end of the month, we have an official serial killer on our hands.

The questions remain, though—who is our mystery killer, and why does he want his victims to pray?

Should God save them? Should the angels?

Or does our killer think he is sending them to the great big expanse in the sky, to heaven? Does he think he is making more angels for God's so-called army of righteousness? Only time will tell.

I sat back, staring at the last paragraph. The article was perfect, but I didn't have a title yet. So far, the police and the news stations had only called the killer the perpetrator. They didn't call him a serial killer yet, because there was only one found body. It wasn't to say he'd only killed once, but in the eyes of the public, he was just a killer.

Somewhere, deep down, I knew he was more than a killer. I knew beyond a shadow of a doubt he was a serial killer, that he would kill again. I felt it in my bones, a sick and twisted promise of blood and chaos.

I needed the blood and the chaos, because it made me feel alive.

No, this article had to have a good title, and the killer had to have a good name.

I read the last paragraph again, and then, kind of like magic, it came to me.

The Angel Maker.

Chapter Thirteen - Lincoln

I couldn't believe Ed wanted to see her again so soon. He was obsessed, had to be. There was no other explanation for it. Yes, her cunt was tight, but a nice pussy wasn't all she was. Those fucking eyes. Those eyes that made me want to gouge my own pair out just so I didn't have to look at them. I still hated her eyes, and I didn't understand Ed's fascination with her.

It would pass. It had to pass. If it didn't…I didn't want to think of what it meant.

Beneath the hidden psychosis, Ed was a romantic at heart. It was something about him I thought both was annoyingly ridiculous and kind of cute—in a more ironic way than an actual cute way—and I'd long since learned it was not something I could change about him.

He never felt full, never whole, and he misappropriated the feeling with needing someone else steady in his life. The truth was, he was just as fucked in the head as I was, and no matter who came into his life, he would never be whole. He was cracked and broken, held together by some dollar store, cheap ass tape. No cunt or dick could fix him, Stella's included.

I tried to make him realize this for the last day and a half. All throughout work, I texted him, trying to be the reasonable one, trying to dissuade him. Inviting Stella into our home again, especially so soon after first having her, would not end well.

In fact, when Ed got a little ahead of himself, the objects of his obsessions always ended up dead.

Hmm. Maybe that'd be a good thing. Stella dead— I kind of liked the thought. At least then I wouldn't have to worry about her or her hold over Ed, at least then no one would ever have to stare into her eyes again.

Yeah, I just couldn't get past those fucking eyes.

Ed would not be dissuaded, which was how we wound up at the bar he'd stalked her to the other day. I had a feeling if Stella found out how much he really did know about her, she wouldn't want to let either of us close to her again. He'd pretty much cyber-stalked her for the last twenty-four hours.

If she realized how much he knew, it could very well be another good way to get rid of her. I filed it away in my mind, knowing murder wasn't always the best solution. It was fun, but sometimes killing someone would just draw too much attention to Ed and I. We had to be careful.

We were early, arriving there before Stella, and as Ed ordered a drink, I looked around the bar. A Thursday night, yet it was packed. It wasn't dubbed Thirsty Thursday for no reason, I supposed. There were some prime targets tonight, too. It was a good thing I drove separately—I'd keep an eye on Ed for a little while, but the entire night was not on me. Ed liked watching, but tonight he could have his freaky-eyed chick to himself.

I noticed a few women, crowding around each other off to the side of the bar, where the booths were. Mid-twenties to early thirties. They all wore tight clothes, and most of them had tits to die for. I could hear them laugh all the way across the bar. I would gladly take a few of them home, but I knew it was harder to pry apart a group.

Plus, if the one who broke apart from the group didn't come home, they'd know. They'd remember me.

Odds were, they'd remember me, even if I didn't take anyone home tonight, because I had that kind of face. Cripplingly handsome, cold in the way that made all the women crazy for me. But if I took a loner home…well, do the math.

They'd remember me, but they wouldn't remember her. She'd be just a nameless face in the bar.

My eyes scanned the whole place, and almost instantly I spotted a prime target. A woman, tears in her eyes, drowning her sorrow over half a dozen beers. Odd choice for a preppy young thing like her; she couldn't have been much older than twenty-one. Barely legal. A college girl down on her luck. Broken up with a boyfriend, maybe?

Regardless of what got her here, she was here. She was sad. And, most importantly, she was alone.

And she was pretty.

Blonde, her hair long and straight. Big eyes and big tits. Thin but curvy. Oh, fuck. She was perfect.

"I think I see someone I'd like to get to know better," I said to Ed, eyeing her up. "She looks like she could use a pick-me-up." I was slow to smile. It was a calculated, cold smile, but it was one that usually fooled most people.

People were fucking idiots.

"I don't care what the fuck you do, Lincoln," Ed said, giving me a glare. "I just don't want you to interfere with Stella. I know you think I'm obsessed, but she's different than everyone else, I can feel it."

I held in a groan. It was not the first time Ed had made a declaration like that, and it wouldn't be the last. He flicked from one obsession to the next with alarming ease.

"All right," I eventually said. "I'll leave you to it." I ordered a beer and pushed myself away from the counter, confidently heading toward the girl trying to hide her tears in the corner of the dimly-lit bar.

The girl looked up at me, her eyes rimmed with smeared black makeup, and for a quick, fast moment, her stare reminded me of Stella's. Not because this chick had two different colored eyes. Hers were both a deep blue, but it was the same blue of Stella's right eye.

Damn it. I was mad at myself for even knowing that.

"Is anyone sitting here?" I asked gently, taking on my kind, warm voice. The kind of voice that people fell for, that women swooned for. This girl might put on a show right now, but she'd fall for me just like they all did.

She shook her head, swiping at her eyes after meeting my stare. Probably thinking *oh, shit. He's hot.*

And I couldn't blame her, because I was, and I knew how to use my looks to my advantage, just like I knew how to do a lot of other things.

"Mind if I join you?" I asked, waiting for her nod before sitting across from her. She'd taken the farthest corner booth. From where I sat, I could see the bar counter perfectly, which was good, because even though I wanted to get lucky, I had to keep a relative eye on Ed. The rate he was going, he'd propose to Stella before the end of the week, and there were a million reasons why I couldn't let that happen.

I turned my full attention back to the crying chick, who wasn't exactly crying anymore. She was probably busy wondering why the hell I was here, sitting with her, when I could have literally any other person around, men included.

What could I say? My looks were universal.

"What's your name?" I questioned, watching her long, thin fingers trace the round top of her glass. Hands like that looked really nice wrapped around my dick.

"Jessica," she whispered, her voice cracking.

Jessica. Not a bad name, but not too a unique one, either.

Fuck. Not like I wanted uniqueness. I didn't. Right now I just wanted a good fuck, an easy one. While Ed pranced around with his new toy, I wanted to be balls deep in Jessica, fucking her so wildly I completely forgot what was so aggravating about Stella's eyes.

"Jessica," I repeated her name softly, "why is a pretty girl like you sitting all alone in a bar like this, crying?"

I knew how the game was played, and I knew I'd get Jessica to come home with me. I'd offer to get her mind off her ex-boyfriend for a night, which was all she wanted anyway when she came here and decided to heavily drink.

In ten minutes, I had Jessica laughing and blushing, and the sound of her laugh was almost enough to distract me from the woman who walked in the bar at seven o'clock sharp, like some kind of stupid fucking timekeeper.

Stella.

Even though she wasn't my obsession, my eyes left Jessica's for a moment, watching as she made her way to the bar, where Ed sat, waiting for her. She wore leggings that hugged her body, leaving nothing to the imagination—which I didn't mind. If there was ever a fan of leggings, it was me. Her hair was down and curled a bit, and I couldn't help but picture myself running my hands through it, pulling it back and...

No. I was with Jessica right now. If there was to be any hair-pulling, it would be done with bleached yellow locks and not Stella's dark brown.

At the bar, Ed pointed to me, and Stella turned her head slightly, her mismatched eyes locking with me, even from across the bar. She made not a single expression at me, like she couldn't care less if I was with someone else—which was more than all right with me, because I wasn't with Stella. It wasn't like I was committed to the chick. She'd just been a lay, a surprising one at that.

And a hateful one.

Those fucking eyes...

I focused on Jessica again, reminding myself not to get caught up in whatever Ed was doing. I would make the girl across from me feel like a queen for a night, and then never see her again.

Okay, that was a lie. I'd make myself feel like a king, not vice versa. *I* was the important one here, not Jessica. Fuck Jessica.

Fuck Jessica, and fuck Stella. Fuck Ed too, for making me go through this again and again.

Turned out, Jessica was either giving it away for free, or she'd already had a few too many. My bet was on both, because soon enough, she'd come around the table and sat beside me, scooting me in further. I was now tucked between the bar's wall and a lithe, well-chested girl who looked like she wanted me to fuck her into oblivion.

It was one thing I could definitely do.

Once she moved onto my side of the booth, she was all over me. Her closest leg draped over mine, one of her hands grasping my upper arm, squeezing me. I heard her inhale when she felt how muscular I was. For some reason, women always did have a thing for muscles. Maybe it made being held down even better.

"You're so big," Jessica giggled out, stroking my arm as if she hadn't quite gotten enough of my bicep yet. Her other hand snaked its way between my legs, rubbing my dick over my pants—it was already getting hard, just by her being so close and knowing I was going to take her home. Her touch only hardened it further, and I let out a long breath.

Not that I wasn't an exhibitionist, I liked performing in front of an audience as much as anyone possibly could, but this was a public place where the cops could get called. Even though I was a cop, every situation was better without any uniforms.

"You're big everywhere," she said, slurring her words a bit after rubbing my crotch. Jessica waited not a second longer to ask, "You want to get out of here? I'm done crying over that asshole. You are just the distraction I need." She giggled, pretending to sound innocent, as if her one hand still didn't cup my hard cock through my jeans.

Oh, Jessica had no idea what mess she was getting into tonight.

Despite knowing I had to focus on Jessica if I wanted my sanity to survive the night intact, I found myself glancing over to Ed and Stella. They looked…close. She sat next to him, less than a foot from him, sipping on something while he leaned closer, talking with a dimpled, boyish grin.

Fuck them.

I didn't need them.

Giving Jessica an easy smile, I said, "We can go to my place, unless you have somewhere else in mind?" I'd found it was always best to offer; it let the women think they were the ones in charge when in reality, the opposite was true.

She was all too easy to please, judging from her brilliant white smile. "Your place."

I assumed it's what she would choose, because in all odds, her place probably reminded her of her ex. Getting fucked while staring at pictures of her ex was not her idea of a good time. I'd show her soon enough what my idea of fun was. Jessica had no idea what was headed her way.

She scooted out of the booth first, and as I got to my feet, I had to adjust myself, grateful the lights were dim in this corner. My erection wouldn't be obvious, and once we got outside and in my car, it wouldn't matter at all.

Within minutes, we were on the road, Jessica utterly oblivious to where we were headed. I didn't even see her reach for her phone once—meaning no one knew where she was, where she went, and where she was going. The perfect basement candidate, but I didn't want her chained up downstairs.

I wanted her naked and in my bed, and I wanted to block out all thoughts of Stella.

Once we made it to the house, I parked the car in the garage and practically dragged Jessica inside. All the while she giggled, letting me drag her by the hand as if she was a child I was about to punish. In a way, she would be punished—but she'd enjoy it. She'd enjoy it almost as much as I would enjoy her.

We went upstairs, directly into my room. Jessica was more than willing to yank off all of her clothes and kneel before me, working on my jeans with an eager look in her eyes. Her body was tight and young, flawless and pale. The kind of body most women today wished for, skin tone aside. And her breasts were bouncing and rounded, her nipples pointed and pink. She had a body to die for, and I looked forward to fucking her brains out.

She pulled my dick out, the innocence completely lost in her gaze the moment she viewed my thick member. And then she went to work—she was very eager to please, using her tongue and her hands together in a way that told me she'd done this many times before.

Practice made perfect, right? It went for everything—giving head, getting fucked, even killing. Yeah, there were some things that could only get better with practice.

Though Jessica knew how to work me, I needed to be in control, so I fisted her hair and moved my hips, pushing my dick further in her mouth. Oh yes, she had done this many times before; she didn't gag at all. She'd take whatever I gave her, and she'd be thankful for it. She'd walk out of this house grateful for the chance to be with me, even if it was only for a night.

One night.

I didn't do relationships, for obvious reasons.

I set the pace as I fucked her mouth, practically pulling her hair every time I thrust my hips. Jessica took it like a good girl, and she'd be rewarded; I didn't often tie them to my bed like Ed liked to. Sometimes I even let them be on top.

Jessica…was clearly a bottom.

My muscles tensed, and I felt it coming, but I didn't stop. I kept thrusting deeper into Jessica's mouth, pushing my hard dick down her throat as my balls tightened. Sticky white cum shot into her mouth—at that, she gagged, but only because it'd been building up since the bar. The longer my release was delayed, the larger the load was.

When my dick was spent, I took a step back, pulling out of her mouth. Her lips were red, saliva dripping from the corners of her mouth. Jessica said nothing, and I watched her throat swallow every last drop I'd sprayed in her mouth. A greedy little bitch she was, and tonight I would give her more than she could handle.

I took her by the shoulders, helping her up and pushing her to the bed. She crawled atop the sheets eagerly, and I watched her spread her legs as I quickly undressed myself. I could see the slickness between her legs, and I knew she was ready for me.

Once I was free of every piece of restricting fabric, I crawled over her, holding myself above her. Her big blue eyes looked at me, looked at my body, and she dragged her hands all along me, taking me in. They always obsessed over the muscles, almost like I was some manly specimen they never thought they'd see in real life. I couldn't blame them. I was practically godly.

I brought my mouth to hers, nipping her lip and making her moan as one of my hands traveled between her legs. Oh, fuck. Jessica was dripping for me. So fucking wet. I couldn't keep myself from her for long. Moving my mouth downward, I took in a nipple, sucking and tickling with my tongue, gauging her body's reactions to my movements. It was an annoying habit of mine.

Even during sex, I was always calculating. Always thinking. Never could I just shut my mind off.

Without so much as a warning, I broke away from her nipple and pushed myself inside of her. My dick needed no positioning, no help to find her entrance; her pussy was slick and ready for me, and she felt good around it. I watched her arch her back as I entered her, heard her inhale sharply, as if I filled her up like no man had ever filled her before.

I fucked her.

It was hard to say how long I fucked her—I could go for a while since she sucked my dick dry—so it could've been minutes later or it could've been an hour later when I heard footsteps in the house.

Beneath me, all red-skinned and sweaty, Jessica whispered, "Roommate?"

I met her eyes, hardly able to mutter, "Yes."

As Jessica laughed and made the joke about asking my roommate to join us, whether my roommate was a guy or a girl, my thrusting slowed. Stella was with him, I knew. Ed's obsession. He'd fuck her across the hall while I fucked Jessica.

Why couldn't that be enough for me?

Why, suddenly, did the blueness of Jessica's eyes bother me?

Why—for a split fucking moment—did I imagine it was Stella underneath me instead?

A sort of growl left my lungs, and I glared down at Jessica, moving my stare away from her eyes, to her lips. To the lips that had been around my cock not too long ago, but with the current state of my mind, it was hard to remember.

"Close your eyes," I harshly whispered, needing to not see a pair of blue eyes under me. Apparently my mind associated blue with Stella now, and I did not want to think of that bitch while I fucked Jessica. I didn't want to think about Stella at all.

She wasn't *my* obsession.

Jessica let out a giggle I was sure she thought was adorable and girlish. "What?" She blinked, those fucking blue eyes refusing to look away from me. Even though I wasn't staring at them, I could feel them.

I could feel them like they could stare at my soul, like they knew how fucked up I was. Like the color of her eyes knew everything.

Stella knew everything.

Rage took me, and I let myself be blinded by it. I barely knew what I was doing as I brought my hands to Jessica's neck, curling my fingers around her throat. She chuckled at first, thinking I just wanted to get a little rough, but when I kept squeezing, when I refused to let go, even as her arms started to flail and hit me, she knew then she'd made a mistake by coming home with me.

All I'd wanted was a good lay. All I wanted was some nice cunt to get my mind off Stella—everything out of Ed's mouth the last two days had been nothing short of a Stella biography. Stella this, Stella that. I was sick of Stella, and I was tired of picturing the weirdness of her eyes, especially her damned blue one.

Why didn't Jessica just close her fucking eyes?

Her skin started to turn red, and then her face turned purple. My grip was so iron strong it blocked the blood flow to her brain. Her thrashing legs and arms slowed, and I watched her eyes glaze over as her limbs fell to the bed, motionless. Those damned blue eyes didn't seem so lively when they sat inside the skull of a dead girl.

I moved my gaze to the side, slow to withdraw my hands from her neck. My dick was still inside her, and it was still hard, aching with the need to be released again. I couldn't keep fucking Jessica. I wasn't a necrophiliac, so I pulled out of her and whispered a single word as I stared down at the dead girl on my bed.

"Fuck."

Chapter Fourteen - Stella

I supposed I could've had Edward pick me up at the house, but I still wasn't sure if I wanted him to know where I lived. There was something off about him, beneath the dimpled smiles and the easy way he had with me. I knew he was hiding something, and I desperately wanted to know what.

Guess I was drawn to the freaks.

I met Edward at the bar right at seven, and I instantly felt Lincoln's presence too. It didn't take me long to see he sat in a booth with another woman—a college girl from the look of her. But it was fine. I didn't care. I didn't think I liked Lincoln as much as I liked Edward. My feelings were…hard to differentiate, because I'd never had feelings like them before.

So for the short while Edward and I remained at the bar, I focused on the man beside me, completely ignoring the one with other girl. I definitely ignored Lincoln as he and the girl sauntered out of the bar, slipping out into the dark night air without so much as a word to Edward.

"I was surprised you wanted to see me again," Edward was busy saying, his stare watching me, waiting for my reaction. As was usual, two dimples sat on his cheeks, a weapon he probably used to disarm his conquests.

I, I realized, was just another notch on his bedpost. Why did the thought bother me so much?

"Why?" I asked, sipping my pop.

"Sometimes I can go a little overboard," Edward spoke with a brilliant, dazzling smile. He was a handsome man, and his looks would make anyone's stomach flip. Even mine. "I was worried I scared you off."

"It takes a lot to scare me off," I said, eyes falling to the bar counter, at the chipped and dirty wood. "I don't scare easily." The truth.

We went on for a few more minutes like this— Edward trying to pry into my mind and find out why I was so tough when my body was practically the size of an eighth grader. I knew he probably thought I should scare easily, considering my size and the fact I was a woman in today's age, where rapes and murders happened all the time and were constantly on broadcast, no matter what the station. Good news was a thing of the past.

Edward couldn't possibly realize how much I didn't fear death or pain. Pain was…almost elusive to me. I hardly felt it. And as for death? Death came for us all eventually; why bother fearing it when it would come anyway?

And why would someone so fascinated with death and the macabre fear it? I was one of the few who welcomed it, and it showed in my writing. If I was a crybaby about those things, my articles would be stilted and just like the rest of the news.

As much as my parents would scold me for it, I would welcome death with open arms if it came to me.

It didn't take too long for Edward to suggest we leave the bar and go back to his place for some quiet time. I knew he didn't exactly mean quiet time in the strictest of sense, but I agreed with him. It was why I wanted to see him again—he'd made me feel things I never felt before. He made me feel alive, like I wasn't living a lie.

We were silent as we got into his car and drove off. As Edward drove, I leaned my head on the window, watching the scenery fly by. I couldn't help but wonder if my killer was out there somewhere, taking his next victim, mutilating their body and making them pray to whatever God they believed in.

My killer.

I probably shouldn't reference him like that, but it just felt right. If he wasn't my killer, whose was he? None of the news stations would do him the same justice I would in my writing. None of them would understand him.

I wished...I wished I knew who he was. Not so I could tattle to the cops on him, but so I could watch his evolution, dig into his past. So I could learn more about my Angel Maker.

We were at his house soon enough, and I noticed Lincoln's car was already in the garage when we pulled in, which meant he and his co-ed were in the house, getting down and dirty with each other. Jealousy was not something I normally felt, and I didn't feel it right now either.

I was a bit mad, though. A little angry.

It would be difficult for me to pretend not to be, but it's what I tried to do as I followed Edward inside and trailed up after him on the stairs. I did not toss a peek at the closed door across the hall, knowing Lincoln and the girl were behind it. I did my best not to focus on the feminine moans coming from the room.

I should let my anger go, because I wasn't here for Lincoln. I was here for Edward.

As Edward closed the door behind him, he said, "It's just going to be you and me tonight, Stella." Like he was warning me Lincoln was busy. I wanted to say something back to him, something snarky, but all I could do was shrug when his sapphire eyes returned to me.

It was the same game as before—Edward gave me orders, and I had to listen, otherwise I'd be punished. I was curious as to what his punishments would be, but I was still too willing to listen and go along with anything he said. Being subservient was apparently in my nature; Edward brought it out in me.

This time was a little different though, for Edward had me take off *his* clothes, first. And then he had me touch him, told me where to press my lips. His chest, his stomach, his thighs and then, just when I thought he was going to make me do something I'd never even thought about doing before, a blowjob, he ordered me to stand up and take off everything under my waist.

My shirt and bra would stay on for now, which was fine. Whatever game Edward wanted to play, I was more than ready to take the board.

I shivered when Edward started to tie me up, my body craving things I never knew it wanted. I wanted Edward inside of me. I wanted him to touch me, to need me. I wanted all of this and more, things I could never put into words aloud.

"What do you want?" Edward asked, kneeling over me, between my spread legs. His dick was hard and ready, sticking straight out, the veins in its side throbbing. He was all I could see, and in this moment he was all I needed.

His body was not quite flawless, meaning there were scars here and there, some of them long and white and risen against the flesh around it. Almost like he'd been cut. The scars were too clean and straight to be anything else. I hadn't noticed them the first night we were together, too wound up in myself and the fact I was about to lose my virginity to a stranger. I should've known there was more to him.

Edward had a darkness around him. His darkness just wore a better mask than most.

Beyond the scarring on his body, he was tall, thick, and manly. He'd told me he worked as a chef at some hoity-toity restaurant a good ways away, and I couldn't help but wonder how a chef got a body like that. All the rigorous sex in the world would never lend to a body like that, meaning he had to work out. I couldn't fault him for it, because his muscles looked good.

When I said nothing, almost speechless at the sight of him above me, he came down, grabbing my face with a passion that I knew only further hardened his already-erect dick. I knew he liked having the power, and I barely blinked when he growled out, "I asked you what you want, Stella. *Tell me what you want.*"

He whispered the last part with fervor, and for a moment, I closed my eyes and let his masculine, tough voice wash over me, allowed myself to bask in the feeling of his hand gripping my cheeks and my chin with an intensity that was sure to leave a bruise.

What did I want? Oh, there were so many things, so many things I knew he would have no interest in.

I wanted to be normal, to not feel like I was going through life like a zombie. I wanted to feel things. My life was like a movie I sat back and watched; I was a passenger. I wanted to be the pilot. I wanted more, so much more out of this life.

But I settled for saying what I knew he wanted to hear, "I want you." His fingers did not loosen on my cheeks; if anything, their hold only tightened. Meaning my answer was not good enough.

"What do you want me to do?" Edward whispered, his other hand traveling up my shirt, beneath my bra, wordlessly daring me to react.

I didn't, even as his fingers tweaked my nipple over and over. I only said, "I want you to fuck me. I want to feel you inside of me. I want you to fuck me so hard I forget my own name." Okay, so it might've been a challenge in a way, but I knew it was one Edward would rise to.

A man like him would not let words like that go. He would take the bull by the horns and ride it.

Or, more specifically, ride *me*.

Edward said nothing before he pushed inside, and I held in a gasp, having almost forgotten the feeling of a dick inside of me. Such a strange thing, feeling so full. Even stranger, wanting to be fuller. Craving more like a druggie on heroin.

As Edward plowed me, I couldn't help but wonder why he didn't use the leg restraints. I saw them sitting on the corners of his bed, and I knew they saw use. He wouldn't have them otherwise. Why did he not use them on me? Did he think me too fragile, too weak to stand them? The other night, he'd mentioned going slow with me—how many times did he anticipate having me here?

My thoughts were blocked out by the sounds of sex. Wet and slick, Edward was able to pump inside me again and again, and I just took it. My shirt and bra were still on, which meant he had nothing to watch but my face as he fucked me, nothing but my expression to go on.

What an adorable fool. I was the master at holding back my expressions.

But I didn't want to seem cold, so every now and then I let out a moan, a deep-throated groan that told him I enjoyed this perhaps even more than he did. He wasn't fucking a dead body. I had to be in this at least a little.

"You are so tight," Edward muttered, his eyes sparkling with lust and desire, his body coated in a thin sheen of sweat. My body was much the same way, I realized. I felt hot—thanks in part to half of my clothes still being on. "Why do you feel so good, Stella? It's like your pussy was made for me."

I had no idea how to answer him, or if he even wanted an answer, mostly because I felt the same. My body was his; he could use it however he wanted. I was more than willing to give it to him however and whenever he needed.

Edward's torso bent, and he finally released my face, moving his hand beside my head as he pressed his nose against mine. Being so close to him, I had to close my eyes, and I focused on the feeling of his body heat against mine, even if I had a layer of clothes between our chests.

"You're mine now," he whispered urgently, desperately.

Mine. Like I had been claimed. Like he could claim me. In a way, I suppose he was, both with his words and with his dick. And maybe it was because his thrusting grew faster, or maybe it was the tone of his whispered words, but I felt something heated growing inside of me. Pleasure in its rawest form, surging toward me in a wave I could not deny.

My body rocked with an orgasm, and I let out a sharp moan, a natural instinct, just as my curling fingers and toes were. The tension that had built inside of my body faded slowly, the orgasm inching to recede even as Edward's dick pulsated inside me. I knew he was coming too, and I could practically feel my sex milking him for all he was worth.

After Edward's trembling ceased, he whispered, "I'm going to fuck you all night, Stella. I'm going to claim every hole of yours as mine and cover you in my cum. I want to make you scream my name before the sun rises."

His words sent shivers down my spine, and I could only nod in agreement. I had work tomorrow, not to mention a weird date with Killian, but I was definitely up for more orgasms and more from Edward.

Maybe all I needed was a firm hand and a hard dick. Maybe all I needed was Edward's words. Maybe, after all this time, I'd finally found where I was meant to be.

Chapter Fifteen - Edward

God, I couldn't describe how much I fucking adored the woman beneath me. I knew she was perfect for me, knew she'd fit in right with Lincoln—the ass was just too busy denying it while he fucked someone else. Soon enough Lincoln would see what I knew before I even met Stella.

She was perfect for us. She had to be.

There was something strange about her that just drew me in. My beast, my darkness, my animal—every part of me wanted her, and not a single part of me wanted to kill her. That was definitely a win, a good plus.

I knew Lincoln probably thought I was obsessed with Stella, and I was—just not in the way I'd been obsessed with people before. Whereas past obsessions were unhealthy, this was good. Stella was needed. Even though I knew nothing about her personal life, I knew she completed me.

Hopefully Lincoln would give her a chance to complete him too, otherwise things would not be so fun in this house.

I gave a wicked grin to the woman beneath me, watching as she slowly opened her eyes. Such pretty eyes, but they were only one part of the picture. One part of Stella. I had to know more about her. I had to find out more.

I was about to ask her what specifically she wanted me to do to her next—which frankly I already had quite a few ideas—but the door to my room opened and slammed shut, and I paused, turning my head to view Lincoln, naked and aroused, and very, very furious.

My brows furrowed, and I did not withdraw myself from Stella before asking, "What about—"

Lincoln cut me off, the fury on his face evident, "Shut the fuck up."

I knew if I didn't let Lincoln have his release, he'd go crazy. I wasn't sure if the girl he'd taken home had left, or if she just hadn't done it for him, but I slowly pulled out of Stella all the same, glancing down at her. She was busy eyeing Lincoln while trying not to seem obvious. I knew she saw his dick was hard and coated in another woman's juices, but she had no objections.

I wanted to bang Lincoln's head on the wall and say *See? She's fucking perfect for us.* Difficult as it was, I held back as I crawled off the bed and gave him space. I watched as he reached for the restraints holding Stella's arms up, untying them with urgency.

Why was he…what the hell happened with the other girl?

Lincoln harshly moved Stella to her stomach once she was untied, grabbing her hips and pulling her ass in the air as he positioned himself behind her. Her shirt fell down to her neck, revealing her black bra. She was on her hands and knees before him on my bed, about to get fucked doggie style, and I was too concerned about what had made Lincoln this way to remind him to be careful with her. We couldn't damage her so early into the night, not when I promised her a night full of sex and debauchery.

Letting out a deep grunt, Lincoln pushed inside of her, shoving the entirety of his thick member into her in one thrust. Stella let out a low, muffled sound, but she didn't ask him to stop. She probably knew that if she did ask, he would not oblige. Lincoln was not the type of man who stopped before he had what he wanted.

"Lincoln," I said, my voice husky, "try to be gentle with her, please. She's not used to your animal." She wasn't used to mine either, but one thing at a time. We'd get there, eventually.

"I will fuck her how I want to fuck her," Lincoln growled out, tossing me an enraged expression as he pumped in and out of her with vigor and ease, the kind of fuck someone only had when they were upset and needed to let off some steam. "Anything in this house is as much mine as it is yours."

I did notice that, at his words, Stella arched her back, allowing herself to take more of him in. She played this game well, I realized; she wanted to be fucked just as badly as Lincoln apparently wanted to fuck her.

Hmm. Maybe convincing Lincoln of her importance wouldn't be too hard after all.

It took me a while, but soon I was as lost in the moment as Lincoln was, running my fist up and down my dick, which had grown rock hard at watching him take her from behind. I wanted to take her together, but tonight clearly wasn't the night for it. Something was on Lincoln's mind, and as soon as the delirious, sex-crazed thoughts left my brain, I'd find out what.

Lincoln's fingers tightened on her hips the moment before he let out a loud moan, pushing as deep as he could go inside of Stella as his lower back tensed. He slammed into her hard, muttering, "You're going to take me, do you understand?" He released her hips, only to grab the back of her head, bending it back, revealing her flushed face. Though his orgasm had passed and his seed now coated her inner walls, he remained inside of her.

I knew it was because she felt good around him, just like she'd felt good around me. He wanted his cock to stay inside her for as long as possible, just as I had, and I knew Lincoln would never admit it aloud. Never show any kind of weakness, for someone would always take advantage of you.

Stella was barely able to nod with the grip Lincoln had on her head, and after she did he let her go, slipping out of her. White cum oozed from her spent hole, but judging from the look on Lincoln's face, he wasn't quite done yet.

He got off the bed, dragging Stella with him, forcing her to her knees at the foot of the bed, her back against the wooden frame. Lincoln glared down at her, his hands tightening into fists at his side. His dick stood in her face. "Clean me off like a good girl, and maybe I'll be done with you and hand you back over to Ed."

With his back to me, I could hardly see Stella between him, and before I could move to witness it, I heard Lincoln groan, which meant only one thing: Stella had listened to him.

Fuck. This was something I definitely had to watch. My balls were already near bursting again. I moved until I got a good view, stopping the moment I saw Stella trailing her tongue along Lincoln's length, cleaning him off. Everyone's juices were on that cock—mine, Stella's, Lincoln's own cum, not to mention the girl he'd brought home, wherever she was. That dick had been milked and used tonight by more than one woman, and Stella didn't act like she cared.

How the hell could Lincoln try to deny her after this? If this didn't prove she was perfect for us, I wasn't sure what would. The other things Lincoln and I got up to when the need came over us…those things we could introduce her to slowly. Killing was an art, and with her articles, I knew Stella felt the same.

Now wasn't the time to worry about it. Now was the time to watch Stella at the mercy of Lincoln.

He let out a sneer as he said, "Shut those fucking eyes of yours. I don't want to see them. I just want your mouth." And then, sufficiently cleaned by her tongue, Lincoln grabbed the back of her head and forced himself into her mouth, causing her to gag. "You better take me in, Stella," his voice paused as he took a ragged breath, too turned on by dominating Stella to talk much, "or this is going to be painful for you."

I knew I should step in, tell Lincoln to cool it, but the sight was too hot. Watching was my second favorite for a reason—it got me raring to go in ways sex couldn't, made me feel things deep in my gut I didn't feel when I fucked someone. I only pumped my hand along my length harder and faster, knowing I wouldn't last long while watching them.

This was not where I had expected the night to go, but I'd take it.

Lincoln fucked her mouth like an animal, and I could only watch for a minute before I felt my body seek its release. My dick ached as white cum shot out, landing on the floor, my body flushed from the orgasm.

I wanted to be inside that mouth, but I knew after this, we should let her rest. At least for a little bit.

It wasn't too long before Lincoln shook, pumping his length into her mouth in short, rapid thrusts as an orgasm swept over him. Bits of white dribbled out of the corners of her mouth, and with her eyes closed, Stella hardly reacted to tasting his seed.

Lincoln pulled out, saying, "I better not see any of that drip to the floor."

Stella responded by running her tongue along her lips, picking it up and bringing it back into her mouth, her eyes still closed.

Tossing me an angry expression, Lincoln said, "I need to talk to you." He went for the door, throwing it open before storming from the room.

Before following him, I knelt before Stella, setting a hand on her arm. Those beautiful eyes flicked open, and I gave her a soft smile. "Take it easy for a while. I'll be right back with some water."

All she did was nod and watch me as I left, closing the door behind me.

Lincoln's bedroom door was ajar only a foot, and I tried peeking in, but Lincoln dragged me to the stairwell, down a few steps until the hallway with our bedrooms was out of sight.

Leaning on the railing behind him, Lincoln crossed his arms, his cock finally growing limp. "We have a problem," he muttered.

"Please tell me it doesn't involve the one you took home. Please tell me she's not up there, dead, across the hall from Stella," I whispered, mostly joking, sizing him up. Not repentant in the least, not that I expected him to be. It wouldn't be the first time he'd killed someone without planning to, however I was *not* happy it had bled into the bedroom with Stella.

"You know me too well," Lincoln said.

I wanted to push him over the railing. It wouldn't kill him, but it just might knock some sense into him. "What were you thinking?" I said, taking a step forward. We were both still naked, but neither of us cared much, not after sharing our first.

"I was thinking her eyes were too blue like fucking Stella's."

I wanted to strangle him now. He killed the girl because her blue eyes reminded him of Stella's lone blue orb? What the hell kind of sense did that make? None. None whatsoever.

"This is the end, right? You're not going to see Stella again," Lincoln stated, hoping I'd go along with it. The man still didn't know how much I needed her, so I had to inform him.

"I am going to see her again, because I want to. I need to. And you need her too, you are just too stupid to realize it."

"She's clearly not healthy for us."

"She's only not healthy for you because you're fighting her. Stop doing that!" I was practically whisper-yelling at him now, because apparently it was a real thing people did in the spur of the moment, just like murder.

"I—" Lincoln was about to say more, but the sounds of a door opening stopped him. "She's—" He went up a step, but I grabbed his arm and tugged him back down. "What are you doing?" he hissed, glaring at me with eyes as cruel and black as his heart. My heart was much the same, only I hid it better.

"I'm letting the pieces fall where they may," I said. Stella wasn't normal—now was the time to put her to the test. Now was the time to see just how fucked up she really was beneath that unique stare.

Lincoln let out an annoyed breath, and I was slow to release him, measuredly making my way up the steps, being as quiet as I could. Almost immediately, I saw Lincoln's door had been pushed open, and I tiptoed closer, peering in from the hall. What I saw…it made me happy in the most peculiar of ways.

When I turned back to Lincoln, who stood scowling behind me, I could only smile. The smile remained on my face as I pushed him into my room.

Stella was…

She was fucking perfect.

Chapter Sixteen - Stella

I couldn't just sit there, while the guys were off doing who knew what. I kind of felt like I had to pee. Being used was…not something I was used to, but I liked it remarkably so. It was like my body craved something it never had before, instinctual almost.

I waited a moment on the floor, wiping at my mouth. I could still taste the remnants of Lincoln's cum, and I wondered if he'd done the same thing to the girl he'd taken home. I'd heard her breathy sighs through the door, so I knew she was here. I also saw the wetness on his dick before he untied me and had me like a dog.

My mind raced. Where was she? Asleep in his bed? Was she not enough for his appetite? Had her stamina not lasted long enough, and he'd needed more to reach his fill? I would not complain about getting Lincoln after, but I was more than a little curious when it came to the girl.

I had to know if she was still here.

Getting to my feet, I tugged down my shirt to cover my bare ass. My fingers curled around the door handle, and I slowly tugged the lever down and pulled it open. I heard the muffled sounds of the guys arguing farther down the stairs, but I wasn't interested in whatever they were saying. I had a one-track mind.

I crossed the hall, pausing before the door I knew led to Lincoln's room. I remembered glancing in it the first night I'd come here with Edward, and I remembered it being dark and gloomy. I stepped inside, quiet as a mouse.

What I did not remember was the girl on Lincoln's bed.

The sheets were ruffled and sticky with sweat, a telltale sign he'd been with her moments before coming to me. Her head was turned to the side, away from me, and when I moved closer, I saw the markings around her neck, noticed the way her eyes remained open. A glasslike expression frozen to her face. I knew it even before I was at her side, gazing at her from the foot of the bed.

She was dead.

Tilting my head, I studied her. I wanted to touch her, feel if she was still warm or had already gotten cold, but I knew my fingerprints should probably stay off her body. Her corpse.

She was a pretty girl, prettier than I was. Her hair was a golden yellow, bleached, if her dark roots had anything to reveal. Her body was not as skinny as mine, not as bony, and her chest was large and ample. She was curvy and gorgeous in a way I would never be, and yet she was here, dead, and I stood, still alive, even after my encounter with Lincoln.

As my stare rose to her face, past the dark bruises on her neck, I couldn't help but wonder why. Why had she met her end here while I hadn't? What made us so different? I met her glassy eyes, realizing their color was only a shade or two away from my blue one.

So Lincoln had taken this girl home, fucked her, used her up, and then killed her? Or had he killed her *while* using her? I knew both options were bad, and I wasn't certain which was worse. I also knew I should probably run from this house and call the police, but Lincoln was a cop, so he had to know how to hide a body. And judging from the way he had been able to fuck me so soon after, how he'd acted...I knew.

He'd killed before.

I was in the house of a killer.

Hmm. Maybe I should be more worried.

It took every ounce of my strength to pull myself away from the girl's body, and even after I left the room, I couldn't stop my mind from wandering. Thousands of thoughts raced in my head and I was powerless to stop them.

Lincoln could've killed her after sex and then gotten off again as he did it. He knew Edward had me right across the hall to fulfill his needs. I should feel dirty, should feel something other than curiosity and acceptance—because it wasn't every day you found out the men you'd lost your virginity to were riding the crazy train—but I didn't. My curiosity was morbid and my acceptance was final.

Oh, yes. I knew Edward had to be in on it to some extent, otherwise there should've been shouting, if Lincoln had told him what he did to the girl.

This was such a strange twist to the night; I found myself wondering where it would go next.

Would these guys try to kill me? Was I a thread that had to be cut? I shouldn't be excited at the prospect, but considering my line of work and what I wrote about, to find my end at the hands of killers seemed fitting, even if they weren't serial killers themselves.

What really sucked was if I made it out of this house alive, I couldn't tell Callie about it. She'd freak and call the cops right away; she was the more normal out of the two of us, and she never understood my fascination with all things morbid.

When I stood and moved back into Edward's bedroom, I was met with two sets of eyes. One dark, one light. Both stared at me doggedly, and I supposed my bathroom excuse wouldn't work, especially not if they saw me in Lincoln's bedroom with the body, which they definitely did if they walked past in the hall.

Damn it. I'd been too entranced in her lifeless blue eyes to notice, too lost in my own mind.

They were going to kill me.

Lincoln stood near the window, his arms crossed over his beefy, solid chest. Edward was beside him, though he looked a bit more relaxed. Both men were still naked, and right now they only had eyes for me.

A normal person would've tried to run.

But I wasn't normal.

I stood with my back straight, meeting the eyes of both men. Lincoln's scowl deepened when I met his stare, probably because he hated my eyes. I didn't hold it against him, because he was the first person to ever tell me he didn't like them. They made him think I was a liar. I wasn't, not really.

"You know I saw her," I said, my voice surprisingly even, considering the fact I was staring down my own two angels of death. "And I know you probably are going to kill me now, so...I won't ask too many questions. I just want to know—why her?"

Lincoln's chest rumbled with a ragged, heavy breath, causing Edward to glance at him sharply. It was Lincoln who answered me, because it was Lincoln who had killed her while Edward and I were busy over here. "I killed her because she wouldn't close her fucking eyes, no matter how many times I told her to."

So he killed her because she wouldn't listen. He killed her to be in control. The question lingered though: why did he need her eyes shut? Was it because the color of her eyes had reminded him of mine?

I...wasn't sure if I should be flattered or not. I kind of was.

I asked the only other question I could, "Why me?"

This time it was Edward. "Because I knew you'd be perfect for us, Stella. I could tell by reading your articles that you would complete us." He gave me a dimpled smile, and still, even though I knew I was going to die tonight, his smile gave me butterflies. I wanted to smile back, but I didn't. "And after tonight, I know it beyond a shadow of a doubt. You're meant to be ours."

Theirs.

His and Lincoln's? Lincoln, the man who'd killed a girl because her eyes reminded him of me? I was...strangely okay with it, even though I knew I shouldn't be.

I watched Edward push away from the wall, slowly making his way to me. He slipped an arm around my lower back, pulling me to him. "How could we kill what's been perfectly made for us?"

As a human being, I knew I wasn't crafted for anyone, but I couldn't argue, because I felt much the same way. These two, psychos as they might be, were mine just as much as I was theirs.

Shit.

Edward sensed something was off. "What's wrong? Are you worried about the body? Don't be. Lincoln will take care of it—" At the mention of his name, Lincoln let out a groan, interrupting whatever he was about to say next.

But that wasn't it. "No," I spoke, eyes crawling up Edward's chiseled chest. "It's just...I have a date tomorrow." My words caught both of them off guard. Edward looked shocked while Lincoln looked angry.

"What the fuck do you mean, a *date*?" Lincoln spat out.

"With who?" Edward asked, keeping calm and collected, but I could tell the news got to him.

It made me...content, to know I could elicit reactions like these from them. Even from Lincoln, who could barely look at me because of my eyes. I didn't know these two well, but I knew enough, now.

I couldn't walk away from them, nor could I walk away from the date I had with Killian. He was my boss, and now there was someone out there killing people and displaying their bodies like people in mass, I couldn't get fired.

And, if I told the whole truth, I liked having power over Edward and Lincoln. I liked that I could elicit such strong emotions from them. It made me feel, for once in my entire life, important. Here, with these two, I was more than what I was before.

"Don't worry," I said, "I won't go home with him like I did with you. Believe it or not, you were my first." *And now you're my only*, but I couldn't say that without sounding like I was plucked from a Disney movie, nakedness and the dead girl aside.

Edward's brows came together. "Your first? Your first what?"

When I smiled and told him "Everything," he shoved me to the bed and ran his tongue all along my body. I closed my eyes and surrendered myself to the darkness, to the luscious, sweet sensations of a blissful void.

These men would be my undoing.

Chapter Seventeen - Lincoln

Ed took her home when dawn started to stream through the window. She'd slept like a baby after we'd taken turns with her a few times. When Stella's eyes were closed, it was almost easy for me to forget the body across the hall, forget what I had to do today, before I went into work, to get rid of it.

Luckily for us, my family had connections. They didn't call on me often anymore, but I was still more than able to use their connections to my benefit.

When Ed left with Stella, I worked on putting the body in the trunk of my car. The wonders a man could hide behind a closed garage door. I threw my sheets in the washer and was currently taking a shower.

Something had to be done, I knew. Something final. Stella was like a plague on this house. Watching her bend Ed to her will last night was…I couldn't believe it. Hell, I couldn't fucking believe Ed wanted to keep her, couldn't believe he tested her by letting her see Jessica's body.

I should've killed Stella last night, barged past Ed and gone into my room. Put my hands around that frail, thin neck of hers and squeezed with all of my might. Watched as her eyes popped out from the pressure and blood vessels broke under her skin. I wanted to feel her take her final breath beneath me.

God, Stella deserved nothing less than my hands around her throat. At the rate she was going, she'd have Ed wrapped around her pinky before the week was out—and it was already Friday morning.

Fuck.

Why the hell did I listen to Ed? Why did I stand back and participate last night when I should've been lugging her body down the stairs too? Fuck, fuck, fuck. I wanted to bang my fists against the tile and scream into the water pounding my back. Stella was a snake, coiling around the Garden of Eden Ed and I had built, and I wasn't about to let her ruin it for us. I wasn't about to let her take him from me.

He was family to me, even if we weren't related. Even if I'd only met him when we were teenagers. He was practically all I had, and I thought we had a good system going—bring home our conquests, share them, dispose of them. Bring home our prey, share them, dispose of them in a different, methodical way. Then Miss I love Serial Killers walked in and fucked the whole thing up.

Stella and her goddamn obsession with serial killers.

Ed and his goddamn obsession with Stella.

Me and my goddamn obsession with keeping Ed sane. Really, I was the only one here with a lick of sense. I was the only one who knew what had to be done to fix this situation.

Stella could not continue to be in our lives. She would mess it up more, and I liked my messes just the way they were, and unlike Ed, I had not completely fallen for her two-colored eyes and her creepy, emotionless face. She had a nice pussy, but so did a lot of other women. She was nothing special. Nothing near special enough to warrant Ed's fascination.

I still didn't understand his obsession with her. I knew it had something to do with the focal point of her articles, but beyond that, there was nothing special about her. So what if she was enraptured with serial killers? A lot of people were, they just didn't freely admit it as often or as publicly. Just because she was a lover of serial killers did not mean she was automatically right for us.

And did Ed ever ask *me* if I liked her? No. No, he'd just decided she was good for us and that we were keeping her. I had no say in the matter, no opinions that meant anything. Why the fuck did he just assume I'd want her as much as he did? I couldn't look into her eyes without wanting to blow my own brains out.

Her eyes were like the fucking devil. One told a truth, the other told a lie, and no matter how hard anyone tried, no one would be able to tell what was what. I was never a superstitious person—I was the most logical out of the two of us—but with eyes like that…they almost made me feel superstitious and silly.

Ed would understand what I had to do. He would realize eventually I only did this for his benefit, for his prosperity. We couldn't live a long life if Stella was included, I just knew. She would drag us down, separate us. I couldn't live a life without Ed in it. No bitch, sweet pussy or not, was going to get in between us. Ed would forgive me for what I had to do.

As if it hadn't already seen enough action last night, my dick throbbed, my balls aching as it grew hard. Just thinking about all of the possibilities, all the different ways I could do it, made me excited. In more ways than one. That bitch better enjoy these last few hours of her life, because I was going to kill her.

I had to kill Stella.

Chapter Eighteen - Stella

When Ed dropped me at the bar, I called Callie immediately. I needed to talk to someone, though I guess I couldn't really get into too much detail about what happened last night...and then again this morning, quickly before we left. Lincoln had still looked at me like I'd grown horns, but I was hoping that with time, he would loosen up.

Maybe he'd loosen up after he realized I wasn't going to rat him out to the cops, even if I should have.

Callie didn't answer. I knew it was because she was probably sleeping, so I let it go to voicemail before hanging up. I'd just tell her later, when I saw her. Maybe she'd be up by the time I made it to the house.

She wasn't.

She was still asleep, passed out in her bed, snoring loudly. I could hear Callie's snores even through the walls, and I actually felt a smile growing on my lips as I hurriedly ate breakfast. I wanted to hit the cafe before clocking in at the Tribune, respond to the latest comments on my blog, and of course email Killian the article for Sunday's paper. It would go online tonight, a few days early.

I didn't even shower. I felt rushed, even though I really wasn't. All I did was change, throw on some deodorant and brush my teeth. My fingers were the only comb that ran through my hair, and I grabbed my bag before I was out the door.

I felt...oddly at ease. Oddly happy. Like for once, my life had taken the right turn. Ironic, considering that turn led to a dead body and two murderers, but it was a good turn for me anyways. I wouldn't go back if given the chance. I would stay right where I was, because Edward and Lincoln made me feel things I'd never felt before.

Cheesy, I know, but true.

Within a half hour, I was at my usual table at the coffee shop, sipping a steaming cup of black coffee, nearly burning the roof of my mouth. Just how I liked it. I had my laptop open, sitting on the table before me, my blog open. I'd given a little hint to Sunday's article, and my followers were going crazy.

They loved the Angel Maker. The nickname, not the actual person, since no one knew who the person was yet.

A sensational crime like this, and whatever was surely to come next, I knew he'd have to get caught. A killer who displayed his victims like that craved the limelight, and those who stepped out of the darkness and into the light willingly were always the ones society was fascinated with. Ted Bundy came to my mind first and foremost. Someone who wanted to be immortalized, someone who thought he'd never get caught. Someone who wanted fame above all else. Someone who made himself out to be more than he was.

I wondered then how many serial killers were active in the world, how many had died from old age or disease and gotten away with all of their killings. What use was solving cold cases when new ones popped up every single day, practically every second?

The door to the coffee shop opened, and I flicked my eyes away from my laptop, watching as a man walked to the counter. His gait was familiar to me, but I couldn't say from where. I watched him in between answering comments, waiting until he got his order and went to another table on the other side of the shop. Short brown hair, green eyes. Cute. Maybe only a few years younger than me.

I stared at him perhaps a bit too long, for his eyes darted up, meeting mine. It was at that moment I knew who he was—I'd seen him before, in this very coffee shop. We had a habit of coming around the same time each day.

He didn't like being stared at. The moment our eyes met, he abruptly stood and walked out of the shop. I watched him go, confused and wondering why the heck he would sit down for only five seconds before leaving.

Unless...unless it had something to do with me. Was I rude? Should I not have stared? I know I didn't enjoy being looked at and studied like some science exhibit. Still, strangers met eyes all the time, caught each other staring constantly. Humans were curious by nature, so it was something we all should've been used to.

I couldn't get the man out of my head, even as the time passed by and I packed up and headed to the Tribune. Those green eyes felt familiar in the strangest of ways. A burning need to figure out how I knew him surged through me, but I knew I'd never have the guts to talk to him should I see him again. I wasn't the kind of person who could walk up to a familiar-looking stranger and strike up a conversation about the weather. I was awkward, too much so.

No, the man would have to remain a mystery for now.

I emailed Killian my article for approval fifteen minutes before the deadline. I got to the offices early, which never happened. Most often I had to email my articles while I was still in the coffee shop and run to the Tribune. Today I was weirdly out of tune, maybe because of last night.

Because of the dead girl.

What would Edward and Lincoln do with her body? They had to have a system, considering neither of them had acted too worried about the naked and bruised body while they were with me last night. Almost like this happened all the time.

Was I signing my death warrant by wanting to see them again? Would I be the next one to meet her end at one of their hands? I should probably be scared, but I wasn't. I was almost eerily calm about the entire situation, and that should've rung some warning bells. Mostly for me, because people shouldn't be okay with stumbling across a dead body, regardless of the context.

I was...not normal. There was something wrong with me. There had to be. What other explanation was there? Why else did I feel so empty but full when I was near Edward and Lincoln? It was almost like they completed me—ridiculous, because no person could ever truly complete another. We were all whole beings, just assembled differently.

Maybe I was too different.

We gathered in the back of the Tribune for our meeting. The same old boring stuff was talked about.

157

What the Tribune's goals were for the following week, how we could improve sales in the community, blah, blah, blah. I wasn't really interested in any of it, but I had to pay attention, because this job was how I got most of my money, even if it was part time. And now there was a possible serial killer on the loose in our city, I didn't dare lose this job. I had to write about him. I had to.

When the meeting was over, I returned to my desk, fiddling with my laptop charger near the wall. I couldn't help but overhear the others talking—about Sandy? Ugh. When the hell would everyone get over that washed-up, desperate woman? I had no personal problem with divorcees and middle age crises, but ever since I'd heard her drag Killian into the restroom at the bar and attempt to give him a blowjob, I was quite disillusioned with her.

In fact, if I never saw Sandy again, it would be too soon. Much too soon.

So I ignored the others, glued my eyes to my laptop. I would not be a part of the office gossip, because I had a thousand other things on my mind. More important things than Sandy and where she was.

It was a bit strange, though. Sandy was never one to miss work, even if she was hungover. She always drowned herself in multiple cups of coffee and stumbled around the office wearing sunglasses. I couldn't remember if I'd ever seen her take a sick day, let alone two in a row. Maybe she was just embarrassed about how she'd acted at Killian's party.

But it didn't matter, because I didn't care about Sandy.

Someone moved beside my desk, leaning his hip on it, doing that thing where you half sat/half stood against something. Killian's hazel eyes were on me, his arms crossed. As usual, he wore a button-up shirt—today's color was a dark blue, which looked a little odd with his red hair. His sleeves were rolled up to his elbows. It was an attractive look, I would admit. But it did hardly anything for me.

After Edward and Lincoln, I didn't think any other man could ever do anything for me.

"You ready for tonight?" Killian asked.

"What?" It was when he gave me a warm smile I remembered—we had a date. Right after work. Shit. How the hell was I supposed to focus on him when I couldn't get my mind off Edward, Lincoln, and the dead girl in Lincoln's bed?

Could I cancel?

Hmm…he'd probably hate me if I canceled. I had to suck it up and do it, and then tell him it was nice, but I never wanted to do it again. Do it smoothly, nicely, so he wouldn't fire me after.

I tried to give him a smile, but I wasn't sure if it looked right, so I let it fall off my face. "Yeah, of course," I said, trying to sound enthusiastic. Yuck. Enthusiasm was an emotion I had rarely, usually only when I was doing something involving my articles, my blog, or researching serial killers.

"Good, because I have a long night planned for us." Killian went off on a long list of things he wanted to do with me, involving dinner, a movie, and something else I drowned out. Killian was a nice enough guy; he just wasn't for me.

He wasn't Edward. He wasn't Lincoln. He wasn't what I wanted.

What did I want? What did I need? I wasn't sure if I could put it into words. I needed more than a normal man. I needed someone abnormal, someone who could handle me as I was. If that someone turned out to be two someones, then who was I to deny it?

I wanted Killian gone, so I said, "Well, there's still a few hours before the official start to our date, so will you let me get back to work, boss?" Hoping I sounded fun and lighthearted, I watched Killian's reaction.

He laughed, his nose wrinkling. "All right, all right. Get back to it." He started to walk away, shoving his hands in his pant pockets as he called over his shoulder, "And I better not see you on your blog." He winked, and I was sure the wink was supposed to make me feel giddy inside.

I didn't feel giddy. I felt…bored. What I wanted to do was get out of here and see Edward and Lincoln again. Going on a date with Killian was the last thing I wanted to do. No offense to him, but he was the last person on earth I wanted to spend a whole afternoon and night with.

God, what if he thought he'd get lucky? What if he tried to do what he did at the Christmas party again, only this time I couldn't fake a laugh and get him off? I had a sudden thought then: I could always tell Edward and Lincoln, and they could take care of him.

Look at me, so casually suggesting murder, as if murder was something I thought about all the time, every day and every second of my life. It wasn't. At least, not murders that stemmed from my own thoughts.

Other people's murders, yes. Yes, I thought about those a lot, especially the body found in that basement.

As Killian asked if anyone wanted lunch, that he was eating out, I was caught up in my own thoughts. How long would it be until we knew who he was? Or would he be unknown, even decades later, like the Zodiac Killer? For some inexplicable reason, I wanted to know who he was. I wanted to meet him, to stare into his eyes and see.

See if he was anything like me.

Chapter Nineteen - Killian

I wasn't sure how this date would go. Of course, I knew how I wanted it to go, but how I wanted things to happen versus how they actually happened were often two extremely different things. I was a planner—and I was usually good at planning—but when Stella entered the picture, it was like my mind flew out the window and I lost all sense. I couldn't explain it.

Stella was unlike anyone I'd ever met before. She sailed under most people's radars, and the only thing that drew attention to herself was her eyes, which she was born with and she couldn't change. I supposed she could've gotten colored contacts or something, but why hide what nature gave her? Her eyes were beautiful, the most entrancing pair of eyes I'd ever seen.

I knew enough about her to know I'd royally fucked up at the Christmas party last year. I knew alcohol affected me; I knew once I started drinking, I only stopped once the night was over, so really, I should've known better. Everyone thought I had been unhinged because of my recent breakup with Julie, but I wasn't.

The fact of the matter was that by the end of our relationship, I didn't care about Julie at all.

Long before it was over, I'd met Stella. I wasn't one to believe in love at first sight—more like lust at first sight—but with Stella, I felt it. I knew deep down she was supposed to be mine. We were supposed to be together. I didn't even ask myself why she couldn't realize it, because I knew I hadn't been the model of good behavior around her.

And then at the bar, on my birthday, when I had thought I was finally making some progress, I went and fucked it up again. *Why couldn't I ever catch a break?* I'd wondered, which had then led me into the bathroom with Sandy. But as Sandy had knelt before me and worked to undo my pants, I couldn't stop thinking about Stella, even with my mind scrambled with alcohol, so I stopped her. Eventually. It took a few minutes, but I did.

By the time I was out, I'd seen her talking with some man at the bar. Some stranger. Like he could give her what I couldn't. Like he was different from me. *What would it take for Stella to realize I was meant for her, and she was meant for me?* I'd thought, depressed. It wasn't the first time I had such thoughts, but I hoped it would be the last.

But the truth was, I knew what I had to do, long before that moment.

I had to get Stella alone, away from her laptop and her articles. Had to spend time with her one-on-one to show her that I wasn't a bad guy. I would worship her like a goddess, treat her like a princess. Like a fucking queen. No other man would ever kiss the ground she walked on like I would. Like I did.

It was perfect when she'd mentioned she wanted to see the crime scene. I couldn't have planned it better myself. Offering to drive, going with her, watching her trail around the house, hugging close to the yellow caution tape, had been a sight. She was so gorgeous when she was focused on hunting a killer. A little journalist on the prowl.

Going with her to the coffee shop, finding out where she spent a lot of her time, had been priceless, though I hadn't been too happy to see that green-eyed guy watching her. I knew a lot of people had to look at her, because she was so striking, and I felt strangely protective of her, as if she was already mine to protect.

Soon. She would be soon. I would make it up to her, make her forget my mistakes. And I would swear off alcohol, though it was a little late for it.

Stella hadn't exactly dressed up for tonight, but I didn't expect anything less from her. I knew she was the dry shampoo sort of girl, and I was more than fine with her hair buns and her leggings. I wouldn't change her, and the only reason I'd asked her to stop writing about serial killers was because the owners of the paper had asked me to.

Now, after that body, they wouldn't make another peep for a while. The popularity of her articles would skyrocket, and maybe I could even get her a full-time position at the Tribune.

I'd read and reviewed the article she sent me for the Sunday paper. It was…enlightening in ways I never anticipated. Her mind truly worked differently. I was constantly amazed at her.

And the Angel Maker? What a catchy phrase. I knew it would catch on to the major news outlets soon, which is why I had her article uploaded to the website before we left the Tribune. If anyone should get to nickname this killer, it was Stella. She deserved it, with all the work she put into her articles and her blog.

I would never admit aloud that I'd read her blog, though. I didn't feel it was right. Her blog was her personal space, and until I was welcomed into it, I didn't want to intrude. I would not make the same mistake again.

Stella and I sat at in a dark booth at one of the restaurants in town. The theme of this particular one was the Wild West, and it had pictures of cowboys on the wall, along with spurs and bison heads. I had no idea if the bison heads were real—a little disconcerting if they were—but the bread loaves this place gave out before the meals were amazing.

"So," Stella said, peeling the bread crust off before eating the softer inner part, "what do people normally talk about when they're on dates?"

Honestly, I could just sit there and watch her eat, but I knew that'd be creepy. I was trying my best not to seem like an overzealous, eager boy when it came to Stella. Not sure how well I pulled it off, if at all.

Her words slowly sank in, and I said, "Normally they get to know each other. I guess we're ahead of the game there. Wait a second, does that mean you haven't been on a date before?" The prospect of no one ever taking her out before was startling and, bizarrely, reassuring.

I liked hearing it. It was like she was mine already—though I still thought I saw her leave the bar with that guy. She wasn't that kind of girl, I knew, so maybe they just left at the same time. She definitely wouldn't have gone home with a stranger. Stella was so much smarter than that.

And, anyway, if there was someone she should go home with, it was me.

"People don't really like me," she said. "So why would anyone want to take me on a date?" When I gave her a crazy look, Stella added, "Don't look at me like I'm crazy. I'm not making it up."

I didn't doubt it. "That's just so surprising."

She shrugged the moment our salads came. Another way this place got you full before your entrees came out, but it was okay. I was starving.

"Why?" Her voice was quiet, unsure. This woman needed a confidence boost, and if I had to be the one to give it to her, I would. I would shower her in endless compliments if I had to, until she finally realized how special she truly was.

And if other people didn't see it, fuck them.

"You're amazing, Stella. You're one hell of a writer. Anyone who reads your stuff knows you put passion into your work. You're driven, hard-working, even if you do push your deadlines sometimes," I spoke with a smile. "You're unlike anyone I've ever met before, and I mean it in the best way possible."

"I'm only different because of my eyes." Stella ran her hands along her arms, looking depressed, like she would rather be talking about anything else, anything other than herself. It was almost like she wasn't comfortable in her own skin.

I would change that.

"Your eyes might be a part of it," I admitted, "but not the only reason. The way you talk about your eyes, it's like you hate them."

She slowly mixed her salad, picking out the croutons before eating the rest. "I do."

Now it was my turn to ask, "Why?" And truly, I wanted to know why. They were beautiful eyes, even if they were different from any I'd seen before. By the end of the night, I would make Stella realize different did not necessarily mean bad.

Sometimes being different was good.

If everyone in society was alike, there would be no creativity, no movies or books. It was our differences we had to celebrate, not our sameness. Who the hell woke up one day and wanted to be average, to blend in with everyone else? Who wanted to stand in a lineup and be the exact same to every person you stood near? I didn't, and I certainly hoped Stella didn't. And if she did, I would make her see the truth.

"People only want to get close to me because of my eyes," Stella muttered. "They think it's cool or something. They don't want to be close to me because of me."

"And how do you know that?"

"Because once they do get to know me, they leave." Stella bit her bottom lip before bringing a forkful of salad to her mouth. "I only had one friend through high school, and she's still my only friend."

I nodded, remembering. "Right. You've mentioned her before. Callie?"

"Yeah. Callie has been the only one to stick around."

Pushing my salad bowl to the side, I leaned on the table, wanting to close the space between us. "What if other people tried to get close to you, but you were too closed off to let them in?"

She looked at me then. Really, really looked at me. For a split second, I thought she really saw me for who I was, but then she looked away, and I knew she hadn't seen me. "I think it's hard to find someone I want to be closer to. I'm…weird, Killian. You know that. Stop pretending you don't see it."

"You're not weird, and your eyes are not what defines you."

Stella swallowed, and a tiny glimmer of a smile crossed her face. This smile was a genuine smile, tiny and shallow, but there nonetheless. It was a smile I wanted to bottle up and save for later. Hopefully tonight I would see more smiles, bigger ones.

Our entrees came in ten minutes. I'd ordered a steak with fries, while Stella stuck to chicken fingers, like a ten-year-old. I might've made fun of her for her choice of meal, to which she simply said, "You never know what you're going to get, but chicken? You can never go wrong with chicken." She spoke them like they were words to live by.

I chuckled, feeling the need to reach over the table and grasp her hand. God, I wanted to make her see that we made so much sense, that this was right. Why was she so oblivious to it? What would it take for her to realize Mr. Right was standing in front of her all along? Yes, I'd made mistakes, but I was trying to make up for them.

I needed her to see it.

I also needed to know if she went home with that guy at the bar…for reasons.

"I still can't believe you've never dated," I spoke as I cut my steak. Out of the corner of my eyes, I watched her reaction. She barely blinked, like she had nothing to hide. Maybe she didn't. Maybe it was all in my head.

Maybe I needed to take a damn chill pill.

"Does that mean you've never held hands before?" I teased her. "Never been kissed?" Stella didn't react one bit. Hmm. So maybe she hadn't gone home with him. "Have you ever thought about it? Have you wanted to?"

What I should've done was follow her out of the bar and watch whether she walked home or got into his car—then I could've laid this nagging feeling I had to rest. If Stella went home with him...I would not be happy. I would be very, very upset. Too upset for words.

"It's...complicated. Have I wanted to do those things just for the sake of doing them? Yes and no. I was jealous of Callie in the past, but only because I felt like it separated us, made me even more different. With the right person, I...I would do everything with the right person."

Her words made me happy, made me almost forget about the stranger at the bar. Stella was a good person; she kept to herself. The odds of her throwing everything away and going home with a stranger were slim to none. It didn't fit with her personality. I should stop worrying about it and move on.

Dinner passed in a blur of time, and it was as I went to pay the check that Stella's phone buzzed, and I watched as she reached for it, her eyes flicking across the screen, reading whatever popped up. The plain look on her face morphed into one of amazement, one of shock and wonder.

I knew what it was—what it had to be, for only one thing ever made Stella so happy—before she said, "They found another body." What I did not anticipate her saying was, "I have to go." She grabbed her bag and was about to slide out of the booth; I would've followed her, if I would've paid already, but the waiter hadn't yet come for the black book with my debit card in it.

She rushed out of the restaurant before I could catch her. What I should've done was just leave the bill, but I wasn't the type of man who could dine and dash. The restaurant's service had been good; they didn't deserve that.

Just like I didn't deserve to be stood up for a dead body.

By the time I got my debit card back and scribbled a tip on the restaurant's copy of the receipt, I couldn't even see her in the parking lot. Stella must've sprinted the moment she got outside.

Fuck.

I stood there for a while, in the waning light, watching the cars on the street pass by, stewing in my anger. I couldn't blame Stella, because I knew how she was, knew her obsession. She was drawn to the unknown like a moth to flame. Still, this was not how I intended the night to go. Not at all.

I'd wanted her to realize she belonged with me, and our next stop would've been one step closer to it. I would've shown her how thoughtful I could be, but my chance was taken by the limelight of the fucking Angel Maker and his victims. There was only one way I could ever stand on the same ground as a killer in Stella's eyes, only one thing I could do to make her see.

To make her see me, all of me.

It was a good thing I had a backup plan. It wasn't what I wanted to do, but it was better than doing nothing. I refused to give up on Stella, refused to let her go. By all that was holy and right in the world, I would make her see her perfect man was standing right in front of her all along.

Stella would have to see sooner or later that I wasn't going anywhere.

Chapter Twenty - Stella

I ran the fastest I think I ever ran, across the farthest distance ever, just to make it to the crime scene and see the news vans, the police's flashing lights, and the crowd of nosy neighbors gathered in the street. The moment I got the notification from the local news station, the moment I saw the picture of the house, I knew.

I knew because the house was on a street only a few blocks away from mine. It was a house I passed almost daily. And now it was the second crime scene for the Angel Maker.

As I pushed my way through the whispering people, I couldn't help but have a selfish hope: the body was arranged the same way, the hands bound together as if they were praying as they died. If he had a different MO, then my Angel Maker nickname was useless.

But I needn't have worried, I realized as I pushed to the front of the crowd, against the yellow crime scene tape. I could see through the front windows of the house, giant glass panes whose light was on inside, the body sitting on the couch in the living room, soaked in blood and praying with her hands on her knees.

Fifty feet away, so it was hard for me to see any details, but I saw she was younger. Mid-twenties. Brown hair. She still wore her clothes, though they were soaked in blood, which would indicate this killer was not killing these people for a sexual purpose. He was killing them for another reason entirely—but what was it?

I studied the scene, like the outer crime scenes of grisly murders were my cup of tea. In a way, I supposed they were, but only because of the body and its implications.

This was getting close to home. Where would the next body be found? Was it just a coincidence I lived not too far from here?

The couple who must've been the owners of the house were busy talking to the police. A middle-aged couple, holding onto each other tightly. The wife was busy sobbing while the husband stuttered, "We—we came home from vacation a day early. We walking in and we...found her. I don't...I've never seen her before, like I told you."

"Forced entry?" The cop was busy scribbling something down on a tiny pad of paper. This obviously was not the first time the couple had been questioned, and inside the house, forensics were already busy gathering evidence. Without the light on inside the house, the body wouldn't be visible if the curtain was drawn.

Which it wasn't, meaning the body must've been placed here recently.

"None that I saw," the husband spoke, his voice shaking.

If there was no forced entry, it meant whoever did this either had a key or could pick a lock. My bet would be on the second one, purely because anyone who had a key to this house would be a suspect, at least for a little while. This couple could easily prove they were out of town.

I wanted to stay, but as the sun set and darkness crept over the world, I knew I couldn't. My fingers itched; I had to write about this. An unscheduled blog post would have to do.

Exiting the crowd, I meandered home. Before taking off my shoes, I flicked the TV on to the local news. Another breaking news banner ran across the screen, and as I sat my bag down on the couch, I heard Callie walking in heels behind me.

"What the hell is going on out there?" she asked, too dolled up for a night in.

I barely looked at her as I answered, "They found another body." I pointed to the TV, and Callie let out a groan.

"I do not want to think about murders right now, Stella. I'm heading out with the girls. We're going dancing like we're twenty again." Callie chuckled, although I didn't see what was so funny, because we were only twenty-five. Plus, how could she want to go dancing now? She moved around the couch, slapping my knee. "You want to come with? You're due for some stress relief."

I shook my head, leaning around her to see the TV.

"Hold on. Weren't you supposed to be on a date with Killian? What happened?" Callie's blissful expression faded into seriousness, and she was suddenly so very grim when she asked me, "Do you want me to cancel? I can, if something happened and you want to talk—"

"I'm fine, just go," I muttered. Why wouldn't she just leave already? *Take the hint and go, Callie.*

"You can always let loose and have fun with me—"

"I'll be fine here, thanks." Usually she never even asked me if I wanted to go with her, because she knew I'd say no. What made tonight so different? My date with Killian? I'd already forgotten about it.

Callie lifted her hands. "Okay, okay. I'll go. But if you need me tonight, text me. I'll keep my phone on vibrate."

The instant she was gone, I pulled out my laptop and opened up a blank word document. Inspiration was mine tonight, and I would not let it go until I had a post ready. I shouldn't be, but I was happy about the second body; it meant we were one step closer to officially having our own serial killer. The Eastland Angel Maker.

I lost myself in my words.

Tonight there was another body. I don't have to tell you all how it makes me feel. If you've followed this blog for long, you should already know. I won't say I'm happy someone met their death at the hands of the Angel Maker, but we are that much closer to having a true serial killer on our hands.

It was at a house not too far from mine. I should be fearful, but I'm not. I might be one of the only people around who doesn't fear death or whatever comes after. I'm not religious, so an afterlife brings me no comfort.

What I am is interested.
What I am is curious.

175

What I am is...so many things words fail to describe.

Who is the Angel Maker? Why does he arrange the bodies in a way that begets praying? The two victims were discovered nearly one after the other, but the first had been long dead, locked away and forgotten in a condemned house. This one had been propped onto a couch in a lively neighborhood, in plain view. The second victim was new, recent.

This means our Angel Maker is evolving, coming into his own. I cannot hazard to guess what his next victim will look like, but I know in my heart of hearts it will be one gory, glorious sight. It will

My focus was drawn away from my laptop when I heard something. What the hell was it? I wondered, setting my laptop aside, waiting to see if I heard it again. A few moments later, it repeated itself, louder this time.

Hold on a moment—was someone at my front door, *knocking*?

I was slow to get up, glancing at the time. It was far too late for any strangers to show up, way too late for any girl scouts to come around trying to sell their cookies. Who the hell could it possibly be?

As the knocks grew, I slowly moved away from the couch, to the front door. Inside my chest, my heart thumped rapidly, for I was in the middle of writing a blog post about the Angel Maker, and I'd just seen the body first hand. I was a little out of it.

I peered through the peephole for only a second before opening the door and letting the knocker in.

Lincoln, wearing all black but looking good, pushed inside, closing the door with his foot and throwing the latch as his dark eyes ate me up.

"What are you doing here?" I asked, reflexively taking a step back as I remembered the girl on his bed. Her body. The reason he'd killed her, or so he said, was because her eyes reminded him too much of mine. Edward was the one who kept Lincoln in check, and it looked like Lincoln was alone.

So why was he here?

When Lincoln remained silent, I asked, "How do you know where I live?" This was when I should freak out and try to run, but Lincoln was tall—well over six foot. He'd catch me easily, so what was the point?

"Ed told me," he muttered under his breath, glancing around. From his position, he could see the living room and the kitchen. "Ed knows a lot about you, Stella. Too fucking much." He pushed past me, moving to the hall in the back, where Callie's and my bedrooms were, along with the bathroom. He checked each room, making sure we were alone. "Ed lied to you, you know."

Were his words meant to hurt me? I'd already suspected him of lying. Hard not to do when you come across a dead body and neither of them acted surprised or worried.

My steps were slow and measured as I returned to the living room, watching Lincoln check the bathroom last. He looked good in all black; it matched his hair and his eyes, made him seem bleaker, starker. More intimidating. But I wasn't intimidated.

I wanted him to come to me, wrap his arms around me and smother me to his chest. I wanted to feel his lips on mine, something I hadn't done before. It seemed I wanted many things I'd probably never get.

"He was obsessed with you before he even met you. He followed your fucking blog and read your fucking articles like some kind of fucking fan." Lincoln paused at the end of the hallway, looking quite dominant and menacing as his shoulders rose and fell with a breath. "He followed your coworkers that day, and it just so happened you were already at the bar. He would've found you eventually."

That was…interesting. I was secretly glad I merited a stalker, but I really wasn't so important. "That explains Edward. What about you?"

"I am not like Ed. I don't like you at all, which is why I'm here. I have to end it now, for Ed's sake," Lincoln said, wearing a scowl. It did not take away from his attractiveness. Maybe I was just drawn to the dangerous types. The ones who could kill you…the ones who would try.

I was just fucked up like them, I knew it, because as he spoke, as his meaning dawned on me, my heart fluttered in my chest. Not the frightened, I-should-make-a-run-for-it type of flutter, but more of a God-why-is-he-so-fucking-hot flutter.

He reached into his pocket, pulling out a small switchblade. Its blade was tucked into a black handle, but with a flick of Lincoln's wrist, the silvery metal came sliding out, an omen of what he came here to do.

Lincoln wanted to kill me, to save Edward from me. He didn't want to do this because I'd seen the body of the girl, not because I'd been shared between them like some kind of toy, but because Edward had cared about me in his own way before he even *met* me. I was a threat to the normalcy Lincoln was used to; he thought I would hurt Edward.

I would never hurt Edward, and even though Lincoln could be a bit of a dick, I wouldn't hurt him, either. I wouldn't hurt either of them, even though I knew how murderous they were. They were what I needed, the only people who could complete me. I could never fight them, and now would be no different.

If Lincoln had to end it, if Edward would truly be better off without me, then I supposed I shouldn't stand in the way of that happiness. It wasn't like I was that happy with my life, so I didn't have much to fight for anyway. A dress fitting with my mom and my sister? I'd definitely rather die.

Lincoln took a measured step out of the hall towards me, and I could tell by how tensed he was he thought I was going to run.

I wouldn't.

I inhaled slowly, closing my eyes. Still, after all this time, I was not afraid of death.

Chapter Twenty-One – Lincoln

I wasn't sure what I was expecting when I basically told Stella I was here to kill her, but it definitely wasn't what she did. It wasn't her to relax her posture, close her fucking eyes and breathe in like she was meditating.

And I didn't think she'd whisper out a meek "Okay." Like she was agreeing with me, like she was just going to let me kill her.

What the hell kind of freak was she?

Within a few long strides, I was before her, towering over her. Even at my closeness, she didn't move, didn't open her eyes again. Stella was really going to let me kill her without a fight, which I found both peculiar and infuriating.

I wanted her to scream. I wanted her to fight, to run, to do something. I enjoyed killing as much as the next murderous psychopath, but when they didn't fight? Took away the majority of the fun.

It wasn't like I had anticipated this to be a fun event, though. I knew Ed liked her a lot, but he was too smitten to see she was dangerous for him, for us. This woman was not our missing link—we didn't have a missing link, because there was nothing from us that was missing. We were as whole as we would ever be.

Stella…I wanted to kill Stella for Ed, wanted to end his obsession, but even now, I knew it was too late. I knew the obsession had already taken root. When I went to Ed to tell him Stella was dead, I knew he'd hate me for a while.

His hatred would pass. Eventually he would understand I only did this for him. For us.

I supposed I could keep it a secret, but Ed knew me too well. He would know instantly I was the one behind Stella's sudden disappearance, because I was the one who could take care of the bodies, just like I'd taken care of Jessica this morning, before I went into work. Luckily my family had some ties to the junkyard outside of town, a portion of it no one was allowed to wander. It wasn't the most respectful way to get rid of a body, but it was all that was available to me without loads of money. Money of which my family only paid me if I completed jobs.

I was getting off-track. *Focus*, I told my mind. *Kill Stella, put her body in the car, and leave*. Should be easy, especially with how she wasn't putting up a fight. A shame, really, because I so did enjoy the screamers.

My hand tightened around the switchblade's handle. I could end the woman with a single strike to the throat, but it would be bloody. I could impale her brain and end her that way, save myself the mess.

Yeah, that's what I would have to do.

Stella stood less than a foot in front of me, looking...well, small. She was a tiny thing, five foot tall, maybe. Frail and thin, like she didn't take care of herself, almost as if she didn't care enough to. Her face was gaunt but smooth, without any flaws. She breathed in evenly, not afraid even a little. Her lips were parted ever so slightly, and my eyes were drawn to her mouth, though I knew they shouldn't be.

I shouldn't be staring at her at all. I should be sliding the blade into her skull and ending this once and for all. I definitely shouldn't be thinking about what she tasted like, whether her lips would be sweet or ravenous on mine.

Right now, she was off-limits because I was going to kill her.

I inhaled sharply, raising the switchblade to her face, pressing the flat side of it against her gaunt cheek. A part of me wanted to hurt her before I killed her, wanted to cut her pretty skin and make her regret ever stepping foot into our lives.

But then…it wasn't really her fault, was it? It was *Ed's*.

When I exhaled, I found my breath was shaky, so I spoke in a bare whisper, "I'm going to kill you." But my fucking voice trembled too, almost as if I didn't want to kill her. Which was just stupid, because I *did* want to kill her.

I did. For Ed. For us. For…

My thoughts trailed off when she opened her eyes. Not fully, but enough for me to see the color distinction between the two under her thick lashes. Her right eye, a gorgeous, deep blue, so startling against her pale skin. And her left: an alluring, soothing amber, the very color most brown eyes wished they could be.

Not those fucking eyes.

They would not get to me tonight. I wouldn't let them.

Unable to look down on them, I pulled the switchblade off her face and spun her around, wrapping my arm above her chest, holding hers down to her sides. With her back on my front, I wouldn't have to look into those fucking eyes while I ended her. No more lies. No more two-faced women. No more Stella.

Once more, I pressed the switchblade against her cheek. What the hell was wrong with me? I didn't waver, didn't stutter. I strangled a girl while I was inside her all because her eyes had reminded me of Stella's. I could kill as easily as other people breathe.

Why couldn't I just end it? Why couldn't I flip the blade and ram it into her skull?

Stella leaned her head back on my chest, moving against my pressed blade, uncaring that one sudden move from me would end her for all eternity. She pressed her lower back harder against me, and I'd be lying if I said holding her like this didn't make me want to throw her to the ground and have her right here and now.

I angled my neck down, watching her reaction as I drew the switchblade down her cheek. The flat edge, so I didn't cut her, but the danger, the implication of what was to come, was present, which should've been enough. Any other person would've screamed, would've fought me, but Stella accepted it—and the way she leaned back into me, the soft moan that escaped her semi-parted lips when I moved the sharp metal to her throat, made me wonder if this one was more fucked up than I realized.

Yes, she'd seen Jessica's body and had hardly reacted, but this was on a whole different level. If I didn't know better, I'd say the switchblade against her skin turned her on.

Only one way to find out for sure.

My grip around her chest tightened, and I took my time as I lowered the blade, trailing it against her skin.

Down her collarbone, over her stomach after lifting it to pass my arms, stopping only when I reached the apex of her legs, where I had a feeling her cunt sat, dripping wet, wanting me to hurt her. Wordlessly asking me to sink my blade into her flesh and instill a type of pain she'd never before felt.

I pressed the switchblade against her inner thigh, forcing her legs open. She didn't shake, didn't tremble once—but she did press herself against me further, grinding herself on me, caught between my body and the weapon.

Fuck.

She was driving me nuts and making me hard. My dick ached in my pants, and my mind needed no help in imagining fucking Stella. The woman was crazy. I could see why Ed liked her so much. I...I didn't like her. I didn't need her like Ed did. I wasn't some hopeless romantic who thought he was missing something. She wasn't mine.

But, in that moment, strange and fucking ridiculous as it was, I wanted to make her mine. I craved her the exact same way Ed did, I slowly realized as I moved the switchblade to the area above where her clit lay. She only wore leggings, so I knew she could feel the cold of the blade through the thin fabric.

Good. I wanted to make her suffer a bit, to make her see how badly she made *me* suffer.

Goddamn it. I couldn't kill her. I couldn't. I just...how could I kill her when all I wanted to do was rip off her clothes and have at her like an animal? How could I kill her when I knew she was the drug Ed craved? Something that could look the hunter in the eye and show no fear was not prey. She was a hunter too, just in a different way.

My will was not nearly as strong as I thought it was, and it crumbled away the longer I held the blade against her clit, even faster when she let out a breathy moan, too turned on to realize just how fucked up this situation really was.

It didn't matter how fucked up it was, because we were both fucking insane. We all were. Me, Ed, Stella. We were all mad, only in different ways. She was…well, I wasn't the kind of guy who thought anyone could ever be perfect for someone else, but if there was a person for Ed and I, it would be Stella.

Fucking Stella.

The arm I used to hold her chest to me loosened, and my other hand traveled down, sliding beneath her leggings, touching her bare skin. Stella didn't pull away, didn't move an inch; maybe because of the switchblade I still held at her thigh, or maybe because she wanted me to touch her. Who the hell knew when it came to her? She was…wild and unpredictable didn't cut it. She was different. She was more.

She was so fucking wet.

My fingers slid against her easily, her clit already a swollen nub that wanted more. I pushed a finger inside of her, basking in the way she gasped, as if she had no idea it was coming. Like my finger caught her off-guard. My hand moved along her, and she started to move her hips along with me, despite the blade on her thigh. I supposed I could put the switchblade away—but where was the fun in that?

"You want more?" I asked, my voice the kind of low it only got when I knew I was about to screw someone's brains out. She nodded against my chest, which was good; stopping would be far too hard now.

The hand holding the switchblade returned to her face, pressing the flat edge of it against her cheek, turning her head to the side as I finger-fucked her glorious hole.

"Good," I murmured, "because you're getting more. You're getting it all."

My words, combined with my finger working her, pushed her over the edge. Stella shook in my hold, letting out a cry of pleasure. I held her up, kept her in place with the switchblade, my finger sliding out of her as I went to put all of my focus on the little mound of swollen flesh at her apex.

My dick throbbed, and I wanted to be selfish, to make her please me, but for some bizarre reason, I was feeling generous tonight. Maybe because I came here with the intent of killing her. What a fool I was.

No, I had to show this woman that I was remorseful. I was sorry. That I wouldn't do it again. Tonight, the only person getting on their knees would be me.

I pulled away from her, taking both my hands away from her body before dragging her to the floor. The TV blared a newscast about a recently-found body, and I knew it interested Stella by the way she turned her head toward it, but I would do my damnedest to get her to pay attention only to me. No newscast. No story. No bodies except our own.

I left the switchblade beside her head, needing both my hands to yank her leggings off. Soon enough she was naked on the floor, all of her clothes tossed aside in a pile. Stella was too skinny; I could see her ribs more than I should, but she was a flawless specimen of a woman, even with those damned eyes.

Running my hands up her inner thighs, her skin trembled slightly under my touch and I forced her legs open, viewing her wet sex in all of its glory. I wasted no more time. I bent down, my mouth meeting with her wet, pink folds, my tongue gliding along, around, my teeth grazing just slightly enough to stimulate.

And the sounds she made…the sounds that came from her throat were like music to my ears. Heavenly and harmonious, making me go at her harder, making me insert two fingers this time as my mouth focused on her soft, aching nub. I would make her come for me a dozen more times before I relented.

This was as much a punishment for me as it was a pleasure for her. I'd come here to kill her, after all. I wouldn't go so far as to say Ed was right in everything he said about her, but there was a connection between us, bodily contact aside. She was the right kind of psychopath. The cute kind. The kind that fit in our duo of mayhem perfectly, so he was right about that part.

I took my time in learning what made her squirm, what made her cry out, and what made her squirt. Yes, she was a squirter, when stimulated the right way. How fun. I learned the grooves of her body, paying attention to things I didn't care to look at before, like how her breasts were slightly uneven—but still gorgeous all the same. I inhaled the smell of her sex, tasted her, nipped at her inner thighs long before I lifted my head up to hers.

The TV newscast about the found body was long over. The only thing Stella stared at with those fucking eyes was me.

I still wanted to pluck those eyes out, but I would hold back. For Ed. For her.

Being deliberately slow as I took off my clothes, I watched her watch me. For someone who was so strange, she sure had a sexy sultry face when it mattered. My dick perked up at the thought that this was a face reserved for Ed and me. This was our face, our expression, and no one else was allowed to have it.

I crawled over her, about to say something about her being ready for my dick, but Stella once again stunned me by lifting her head off the floor and meeting me, pressing her lips against mine.

She was kissing me.

She was kissing me, and she started it.

I wasn't sure why it felt like such a huge deal, but it was. I knew it was.

As I pushed my tongue into her mouth and taught her how adults played, I couldn't help but wonder if she could taste her own juices on me. I didn't wipe myself off once. Either way, she didn't care. She was inept for the first few moments, but soon enough her tongue danced with mine, lighting a fire in my stomach. A fire that could only be put out with her pussy around my cock.

I didn't break our lip lock when I reached between us and grabbed myself. I hardly needed to position my dick; it was like it already knew where to go, what hole it had to fill. I did, however, pull my mouth from hers when I thrust inside her, pushing myself as deep in as I could go. She was so wet for me there was no resistance at all. Her body took it in, and her eyelids fluttered shut as she relished in the feeling of my dick pounding into her, how my balls slapped against her ass with each motion.

God, I could go all fucking night with this woman, as long as I didn't focus on the hue of her eyes. Those damn things, I wasn't even sure whether I'd get used to them, but I'd have to try.

Stella squirmed underneath me, her chest heaving with every thrust. We forgot about the world, about the reality of the situation. I nearly forgot all about the switchblade I'd held to her face and between her legs. The only reason I remembered it was there was because I set my arms around her head, blocking her head in with my forearms, drowning out everything else but me. She had to focus on me, just like I had to focus on her. My elbow knocked into the switchblade, and I pushed it aside, needing to feel the flat floor around us, to ground me.

The pressure built too soon. Far too soon. I didn't want it to happen so quickly, but I was powerless to stop the orgasm from taking hold of me, from milking my dick and having my cock release my seed inside Stella. I let out a moan before I could help myself, before I could stop myself, and I felt her hands move to my sides, her nails dragging along my skin.

Oh, fuck.

Yes.

Chapter Twenty-Two - Stella

How many times did Lincoln and I have sex? I wondered, laying on the floor with him. I laid partially on his chest, thick and muscled as it was, which was probably the closest I'd get to cuddling with either him or Edward. They didn't seem like they enjoyed things like cuddling in general, and I couldn't say I blamed them, because until now, I never thought I'd like it as much as I did.

Having never had a boyfriend before, well, I was starting to like a lot of things I never enjoyed before. Cuddling, sex, being almost murdered. That last one especially—the rush of adrenaline that had coursed through my body when I'd realized why Lincoln was at my house, how narrowly he'd missed Callie—it was unlike anything I'd ever experienced before.

It was…invigorating. Like breathing in life itself. Knowing how easily he could've killed me, and technically knowing how easy he could still end my life, it was an indescribable kind of high. I rode the high waves all through the sex, and I still felt tingly in all the places I probably shouldn't.

But maybe that was because Lincoln was breathing evenly beneath my cheek while dragging the switchblade along my lower back, tempting me. Teasing me. The blade was short, only a few inches long, but sharp. As he dragged it back and forth, sometimes in circles, I couldn't help but shiver against him, craving more.

I knew it was a sick and twisted desire, not to mention how stupid I was for wanting a man who'd sooner kill me than admit any real feelings for me, but it seemed I couldn't hold back when it came to Edward and Lincoln. They were my weakness, these two crazy, murderous madmen. They completed me.

What did that say about me?

What did that say about my state of mind?

I'd always been fascinated with serial killers and the so-called dredges of society, but to actually have fallen into bed with the two of them, to willingly give myself to them over and over, knowing what they did, what they were capable of—it meant one thing: I was mad, too. I was just as crazy as they were, only less murderous. Less vengeful. Danger was like heroin to me.

Eventually reality came crashing back, and I inhaled a deep sigh. Sweat and sex still lingered in the air, the telltale sign of what Lincoln and I did for the last…hour? Or two? I wasn't sure; I couldn't see a clock, so I couldn't tell the time. We both should get up soon though, because who knew when Callie would get home.

The last thing I wanted Callie to see was me and Lincoln naked and sweaty on the floor. Not just because it would've been embarrassing, but also because, after everything, I was suddenly so very selfish when it came to Lincoln. I did not want to share him with anyone else, didn't want to find any other women in his bed, whether they were alive or not. Not again.

He was mine now.

Edward and Lincoln were mine.

A similar thing must've been on Lincoln's mind, for as he continued to trace my lower back with the switchblade, he whispered, "How was your date?" He practically growled out the final word, as if it was acid on his tongue, the hardest word he had to speak in years. His voice was still ragged and rough, just like it'd been during our intense, heated passions.

How should I answer that? I debated, but I eventually decided just to say the truth, because I wasn't a liar. Not a fan of lying in general. "We went out to dinner, but that's it. Killian probably had a whole night planned, but I couldn't stay with him, not after I got a notification another body was found."

As I spoke, I felt Lincoln fume beneath me, and I lifted my head a few inches off his chest to stare at him. Why was he getting so angry? What had I said that was wrong? It wasn't like Killian and I did anything. He didn't make a single move on me—which was honestly something I could appreciate, after that fiasco of a Christmas party last year.

"What is it?" I asked, when Lincoln only stared hard at the ceiling, like the drywall held all the answers.

"I know Ed didn't make a big deal about it before, but now…let's just say, for Killian's sake, you best not bring him up in front of him again," Lincoln finally said. "Ed is a very jealous person. I'm surprised he didn't go after Killian when you mentioned it. Then again, he did have work today—"

I tried to picture Edward going after Killian with the intent of murdering him, all for me. All to keep me to himself. To him and Lincoln. I couldn't though, and not because I had feelings for Killian—it was the farthest thing from the truth. I just…I wasn't sure why. Maybe because, even though he was kind of an ass when he was drunk, I liked Killian. I just didn't like him like *that*.

"Killian is a good boss. Edward can't kill him," I said, aware that my defense of Killian wasn't exactly stellar. It was a good thing Killian wasn't around to hear my pathetic attempt at defending him.

Letting out a short chuckle, Lincoln said, "I'll try, but once he gets his mind set on something, it's hard to convince him otherwise." Still, he dragged the switchblade along my back, this time up my spine, and I shivered against him, leaning my face against his muscled chest.

"You were going to kill me," I said slowly, raking my nails across his chest. "Because you think he's too obsessed with me."

"Yes. You're not the first woman he's had his sights on."

I didn't like hearing that, and I frowned against his hot, sweaty skin.

"They never end well. He either outgrows his obsession or I make him realize how fucking stupid he's being. But you…you're not like the others. You're different. Fuck, Stella, I came here to kill you and I ended up fucking you like crazy. I can honestly say that's never happened before."

Tilting my head, I gave him a look.

"What? I'm serious," he said. "I totally get why Ed likes you so much. There's something about you that's different than the others. You're…different."

"So you aren't going to try to kill me again?" The thought was both relieving and somewhat upsetting. The thrill of it was not something I'd be able to compare to anything else, and that was saying something.

Lincoln gave me a smirk. "Don't look so disappointed. Ed could always change his mind about you, and then you'll be on my shit list again."

"And what about you? Do you only like me because Edward likes me?"

"What makes you think I like you at all?"

His words stung at first, but I wouldn't let him have the satisfaction of hurting me. Not only was I not afraid of physical pain, but I also was insanely hard to hurt emotionally. I sounded perfectly normal as I answered, "I know sex means nothing to you, but if you didn't like me at least a little, I think you would've put that switchblade into me a little while ago, instead of having this conversation. Am I wrong?"

As I watched him stare at me, realizing I was right, I couldn't help but feel myself grow warm. Lincoln had done all of this for Edward. God, I wanted someone who would do things like this for me. Not necessarily murder, but it was the thought that counted, right? I had no one. Even Callie didn't really understand me. My family never did. I was alone even when I was surrounded by people.

When Lincoln remained quiet, I whispered, "I wish I had someone like Edward has you. It's sweet, how you care for him." It felt like mush and sap coming straight from my mouth, but it was the truth.

He looked like he wanted to say something, whether to scold me for calling him sweet or assure me of my insecurities, I couldn't say, because an annoying jarring sound entered the room. His cell phone.

Lincoln dropped the arm he had around me, the switchblade against my lower back losing its pressure as he reached for his pile of clothes and dug out his phone from his black pants. He took one look at the caller id and hit the green button, answering, "Ed."

Though I wasn't a part of the phone call, I could still hear Edward practically shout into the line, "Where are you?"

At that, Lincoln shot me a sly look. "I'm at Stella's house."

It wasn't but a second before Edward demanded, "Why? How did you even—"

Brushing him off, Lincoln said, "Oh, you talk about Stella so much, how could I not know where she lived? And you know why I came here. To kill her." So matter-of-factly. So simple, like my life had meant nothing to him.

It clearly meant something, but I didn't think it meant as much as I wanted it to. I'd give them time. They'd had years to earn each other's trust and loyalty. I'd only come into their lives recently, even if Edward had been following my articles and my blog. There was no way I'd worm myself into their lives that fast.

I would try my best, though.

Edward started swearing on the other line, and Lincoln held the phone a few inches away from his ear, tossing me an annoyed look. As if his friend's swearing fit was all my fault. In a way, I supposed it was, but what should I have done? Offered my life on a silver platter? I did that already, and it led to some of the best sex I'd ever had in my life.

Granted, I had nothing to compare Edward and Lincoln's sex to, but I was fairly sure they weren't comparable to the run-of-the-mill, everyday Joe walking the streets. They were a cut above the rest, in every way.

"And why?" Lincoln echoed Edward's question. "You know damn well why." As Edward went on, chatting up a storm on the other line, he added, "Stop your worrying. She's not dead. I didn't kill her. She's a little more…worn out than she was before I got here, but besides that, she's no worse for wear." His dark eyes were on me, twinkling as he said, "The bitch is crazy. Our brand of crazy."

Other women might get upset at hearing the man they just slept with call them a bitch, but I couldn't help but feel good about it. Like I was being accepted into their group, their pack, their duo. It didn't bother me at all.

Lincoln let out a low chuckle, soft and cocky as he listened to what Edward said. "You got it. See you in a bit." He hung up the phone, never once breaking eye contact with me. "Edward just got home from work. He wants me to bring you over, probably to make sure I wasn't lying about you still being alive."

Hmm. He worked late on a Friday night, but I knew restaurants stayed open late, and his cooking—the little bit I'd had of it so far—was to die for, so I knew he hadn't been lying when he told me he was a chef.

Callie would be out late anyway, so there was no point in me saying no. I wasn't even sure if I could say no. Lincoln could take me even if I fought him—which I never would. All I needed was some clothes so I could leave through the front door and not flash the entire world my body, and I'd be good to go.

I gave him a nod. "Let me clean up and write Callie a note, then we can go." I got to my feet and grabbed the clothes Lincoln had torn off me when he'd finally realized he couldn't kill me.

"Your roommate," Lincoln mused, slowly getting up and dressing himself, unhurried in every way. "Is she anything like you? Where is she now?"

"She's out clubbing." I held in a laugh. Callie, like me? Not even a little. Really, it was remarkable we were still friends after high school and college. We were so different from each other, different personality types and different hobbies. But we were still besties, and I wouldn't trade her for the world. I was protective of Callie like Lincoln was protective of Edward. Only less murderous about her. "And no, she's nothing like me. She's...more normal."

Lincoln paused, his pants hanging off his hips, unzipped and unbuttoned. "Fuck normal," he muttered, zipping his pants with a jerk of his arm.

Fuck normal. That was a good motto, one I should adopt.

After dressing myself and quickly cleaning up the mess we'd made with our bodily fluids on the floor, I went into the kitchen and wrote Callie a note. I also texted her that I was heading out; I'd tell her the details tomorrow.

We made the drive to their house a city over in record time. Lincoln was a cop who had a lead foot, apparently. I barely made it past the front door before I was swallowed up in Edward's arms, a hug so tight it stole the air from my lungs. He threw an irritated expression toward Lincoln, who shrugged it off.

The night became ours, although some might argue it had belonged to us since the beginning.

Chapter Twenty-Three - Edward

I could not believe Lincoln was going to kill her. Yes, I was aware my obsessions sometimes got out of hand, but Stella was unlike anyone I'd ever met before. I knew it before laying eyes on her. She was different in the best of ways, and weirdly enough, it took trying to kill her to make Lincoln realize it.

That was what I had to focus on: the fact he hadn't killed her. She'd convinced him, somehow, that by being unafraid of death, of his advancing figure, she was one of us. Plus, from what I heard, the way she ground up against him when he held the switchblade against her was…erotic, to say the least.

God, I wish I would've been there to witness it. Although if I was there, I probably would've stepped in and stopped him, because I couldn't picture a life without her. Now that I knew her, now that I had felt every inch of her body against mine, there was no possible way I'd ever want a life without Stella. I was more than addicted to her and her strangeness; I needed her like I needed the air to breathe.

When Lincoln brought her home to me, I spent the next hour with her on my bed after pushing him out. I needed time alone with her, had to make sure she was okay, that he hadn't harmed any part of her. If he had, if he had marked her pale, pretty skin, I didn't know what I would've done.

Gotten angry? Probably. Wanted to hurt something he cared about in equal measure? Oh, definitely. The problem with Lincoln was he never cared about anyone other than me, which I was fine with. It helped with our lifestyle.

But when it came to Stella, he had to feel something, had to feel close to her in ways he'd never felt close to another woman before. Granted, she wasn't the most normal woman around, but we didn't need normal, because we weren't normal.

Hell, we were the furthest thing from normal. We were a pair of guys living with each other who liked to share every aspect of our lives, even the people we brought home to fuck. Not everyone was as loose about things like that, I knew. Not everyone would understand our lifestyle, occasional murder aside.

Stella was perfect for us. She wasn't normal, either. If there was a woman made just for us out there, it was her. She'd seen the body Lincoln had left in his bed, and she'd barely reacted. If someone could take a corpse in stride like that, she was perfect for us.

She was ours, and I'd make Lincoln realize it soon enough.

Eventually, after I'd made sure she was all right and apologized profusely for what Lincoln had tried to do to her—meaning, I tied her up and fucked her until her eyes were glazed over in a haze from the sex and the orgasms—I let Lincoln in the room.

He was…definitely different than he was with her before. Whatever had taken place at her house had indeed changed him, because Lincoln wasn't as much of a domineering asshole in bed as he usually was. He wasn't gentle exactly, but in his own way, he was. He even looked at her while he pounded into her, right into her differently-colored eyes. Eyes he'd said on numerous occasions he didn't like. Eyes that supposedly made him go mad.

Maybe Lincoln was starting to realize that going mad sometimes was the only way to go. And going mad with Stella? The best.

By the time we were spent, the space between Stella's legs was pink and swollen, used up and sore, but she didn't complain. In fact, she slept soundly, almost snoring on my bed. Her face held the most peaceful expression while she slept, tranquil and serene. It was a look she never wore when she was awake; maybe that's why I couldn't stop staring at her, watching her naked chest rise and fall with each breath.

As I stared down at her, I couldn't help but wonder what had created this woman. What had shaped her as a girl that led her to become this woman. A woman who hardly smiled, who hardly showed any emotion. I knew she had emotion in her heart, because I'd seen glimmers of bliss and contentment when she was with us, so it was almost like she hid them from the world. Tucked away her emotions in a safe place, only letting them out when she knew no one would mock her for them.

Maybe that was it. Maybe she'd been made fun of growing up. Her obsession with serial killers wasn't a new thing, and kids could be cruel. If she'd been as interested in killers as she was now while she was in school, I didn't doubt she was mocked. Years of ridicule would do that to a person. People were awful creatures. It's why I usually didn't care too much when

I killed them, or helped their death along if I was doing a job for Lincoln's family.

And then, of course, I couldn't help but wonder if her parents were supportive. She had hardly any contact with them, I knew, so I highly doubted it. With no support system, how the hell was Stella supposed to grow up and be normal?

But she'd found us. Or, rather, I'd found her, so now it didn't matter. Her past didn't matter; only her future did, because I'd be damned if I let her walk out of my life now that I had her.

The morning hours came sooner than I wanted them to, and I was up before the sunlight graced the windows. I went downstairs and started breakfast. In a few hours, I'd have to go in to work, but that meant I still had some time with Stella. I'd swing her by her house on my way, even though her house was in the opposite direction. I didn't care. It just meant more time spent with her.

As I stood near the stove, I wondered what it would take for her to move in with us. We probably weren't ready for that, but it was something that weighed on my mind. I wanted her here with us. I wanted to come home from work and find her lounging on the couch, wearing nothing but a T-shirt. I wanted to have her constantly, twenty-four hours a day and seven days a week.

Maybe I was going overboard. Maybe it was too much too soon, but I didn't care. I wanted what I wanted, and I wanted her. I wanted Stella to officially become one of us, and living with us was the first step to it. The other steps…those couldn't be rushed. Those would come in time.

Hmm. Maybe Lincoln and I could show her the basement soon…see what she thought of it. I doubted she'd run away. If anything, Stella would be curious, and she'd ask what every single instrument did and what we used them for. Her mind was both curious and morbid, and it was something I adored about her.

I heard Lincoln get up and shuffle to the shower, which meant Stella was alone in my room, asleep. I'd untied her wrists a while ago after seeing the red burns around them. We'd gotten a bit wild last night, but she hadn't complained once. She wasn't the type to complain, which was good. Complaining irked Lincoln like nothing else.

After a while, Lincoln sauntered down the steps, barely dried. He was naked, collapsing onto the couch as he snatched up the remote and flicked the TV on. He never seemed to care much about his nakedness, even when the windows were wide open. It wasn't like we had sidewalks here, so it was very rare that anyone saw him.

Cutting up some fruit to go along with breakfast, I shot him a look. More like a glare, but he was hardly paying any attention to me. "You're lucky you changed your mind," I said, refusing to back down, even when he turned his dark-eyed stare to me. Unlike Stella's one amber eye, which held warmth and a light, syrupy color, Lincoln's eyes were so dark they were only one shade lighter than black. If the grim reaper had a stare, I was sure it'd look like that.

But I wasn't afraid of him. Maybe for a split second, before he'd made my presence known in that abandoned warehouse all those years ago, but not really. Fear was not something I felt. It just…wasn't.

I would go toe-to-toe with the beast.

He raised a single brow mockingly. "Am I?" Lincoln asked, unimpressed. "What would you have done, Ed? Tried to kill me in revenge? We both know I'm the one person in the world you'd never kill."

"You're right," I muttered, unhappy. I was strangely protective of Stella, considering I'd only met her face-to-face this past week. Still, it was like she was already a part of the family. Our dysfunctional, makeshift family of killers, both serial and contracted. "But I am not above torture."

Lincoln let out a bark of a laugh, kicking his feet up onto the coffee table. "You would've tortured me? All for her? Damn, Ed, I knew you had it bad, but I didn't know we were at that level already."

Already. Like Stella was just a phase. Like this had happened before.

Yes, I might've tried to invite women into our lives in the past, hoping they'd be our missing link, but they never panned out. And those women were nothing like Stella. Why was Lincoln so against admitting Stella was practically molded for us? She was perfect. She fit into our lives smoothly and easily, and she was more than okay with being shared between us. What more could we ask for? What more did the bastard want?

I knew he probably wanted no one to join us—he was always so adamant against having a third. There was no missing link in his eyes. We would forever remain a duo if he had his way. Hopefully Stella's presence could change his mind.

Hopefully he wouldn't try to kill her again, because if he did, if he succeeded, I knew I'd snap. There was remarkably little holding me together, keeping my sane face on. The realm of insanity was where I called home, charisma and dimples aside.

"Torture, huh?" Lincoln went on, oblivious to me in the kitchen. "It's been a while since we had to torture anyone for the family." And then, right when I started to wonder whether I'd have to say more, to protect Stella from him, he said something that stunned me: "Do you think she'd enjoy doing something like that?"

Did I…was he asking if I thought Stella would enjoy *torturing* someone?

To make someone bleed, to hear their wails of pain—it was unlike anything anyone could experience, unless you'd done it before. But would Stella enjoy it? I couldn't say. I knew she was desensitized about death, but to go so far as to inflict pain on someone else and enjoy it? I…I didn't know.

I wasn't sure, so I kept my mouth shut, lost in my own mind as I pictured Stella taking a knife to someone's skin, pressing down hard enough to cut through the top layer and let blood gush out in a clean, thin line. Would she smile as she inflicted pain? Or would she only prefer to watch? Hmm…perhaps that was something I could think about today. Something I could plan, maybe.

I didn't want to go overboard, but when it came to Stella, I didn't know restraint. She made me feel everything, and I wanted to give her the chance to experience the world. And if that included pain and death, well, I'd be more than happy to stand at her side and guide her through it.

"I don't know," I whispered, *but you gave me a wonderful idea.*

Before Lincoln could say anything else, Stella herself stumbled down the stairs, letting out a cute yawn before mumbling something about coffee. I told her I'd bring her a cup, and she nodded, running her thin fingers through her messy hair and wandering to the couch where Lincoln sat. She was either oblivious to his nakedness or completely unaffected by it. I wasn't certain which was funnier.

As soon as I gave her a cup of coffee—black, how she liked it—Stella practically inhaled it. Once the cup was half gone, she snatched the remote and flipped channels until she came upon an early newscast. Currently they were talking about the weather, but their next story was slated to be breaking news about the body found last night.

"I'm calling him the Angel Maker," she spoke quietly, to no one in particular. To either of us, to both of us. I paused in my fruit-cutting, watching the awe form on her face. "I was able to see the body last night. He's evolving, becoming more confident."

"The first body was only found a few days ago," Lincoln muttered, frowning. He was not thrilled she'd changed the station on him, but he didn't care enough to switch it back. "No killer becomes that confident that fast. He's either been killing for a while, or he's planned this out." He spoke with conviction, as if he were the blasted Angel Maker.

Which he wasn't. Neither of us were. We liked to kill, but we didn't make a public spectacle about it.

Stella quieted, thinking about Lincoln's words. She was slow to nod. "I think you're right, but that begs the question—what else does he have planned? And who is his audience? Who does he want as a witness? Leaving the body in a house, right near a window…"

I scooped the cut fruit onto three separate plates, focusing on the omelets next. "Bold," I said. "It's obvious he wants someone to pay attention."

"But who?" she asked. "Who does he want to pay attention?" Stella pursed her lips, lips that were still a bit raw from last night's activities. "What if…what if it's me he wants? You found me through my articles, so it isn't too far of a stretch. What if you two weren't the only killers reading my stuff?"

Pausing, I met eyes with Lincoln. I sure as shit didn't want anyone else sniffing around Stella—and that included her fucking boss and whatever guy was her Angel Maker—and it looked like Lincoln felt the same. A definite step up from wanting to kill her.

It was a moment before I said, "It's not out of the realm of possibility. You should be careful. Don't go anywhere alone." I would've offered to spend the day investigating this Angel Maker, but I had work. Plus, Lincoln was the cop, not me.

"Callie's always out," Stella said. "Most of the time I'm alone in the house."

"Then maybe you should stay here," I said.

She shook her head. "No. If this is all for me, I want to see it through."

I stared at her, knowing exactly what she meant. She wanted to see what else he would do for her, how many other people would meet their end at his hands in her name. Stella could very well be wrong, and maybe the Angel Maker wasn't focusing on her—maybe it was all one big coincidence—but it was hard to think that when I'd found her the same way.

What if this Angel Maker wanted her attention because he wanted her to write about him? Most killers today wanted fame, to be immortalized. It wasn't too far of a stretch, even if her theory was grasping at straws, because as far as I knew there was no evidence to point to his inclusion of Stella. The police would've been all over her if there was a connection between her and the Angel Maker.

"Fine, but no unnecessary risks," I said. "You try to be safe, and if you think he's anywhere near you, you call me."

Lincoln tittered, managing to chuckle out, "What a hero."

Stella smiled somewhat at that.

I knew there was nothing I could do to make Stella realize that if he was after her, there were only so many steps he'd take before coming directly for her. If his obsession was anything like mine, it was only a matter of time before he tried to have her, regardless of what she wanted. Although, with her strange thought processes, maybe she would want him just like she wanted Lincoln and I. Maybe we weren't enough for her.

No. I refused to think about it. I would not. I would only drive myself mad.

And right now, we had all the madness we needed with the Angel Maker.

Chapter Twenty-Four - Stella

Too soon was I back in my house, practically collapsing on the couch. I was exhausted after last night, and truthfully, it kind of hurt to walk. Almost like I had an aching sore between my legs. Like a rash that would go away with time. I hoped the guys wouldn't want me over again tonight—because I knew I couldn't deny their request, but my body needed rest. Time to recover and recuperate.

Plus, I had researching to do.

While it was already too late to fix the article going to press for tomorrow's paper, I could start Wednesday's article, or even a blog post.

I had a lot on my mind. After wondering if the Angel Maker was similar to Edward in the way he followed my articles, I couldn't shake the thought. If all of this was for me, if he was doing it so I would write about him, I wasn't sure how I felt. I knew what I should feel, what society would want me to feel— freaked out, disgusted, angry. But I felt none of those emotions. I only felt...curious.

So curious it hurt.

I was just me, after all. I wasn't important. In the grand scheme of things, in the great big world, I was a nobody. Unimportant in every single way, unremarkable even with my focus on serial killers. There were others out there who found them as interesting as I did; I was not alone in that respect, just like I wasn't the only one to write about them. The news covered the crimes and the trials, and documentaries were coming out at an almost alarming rate.

No, the entire world was obsessed with serial killers just as much as I was.

Which only made me wonder if I was indeed the focus of the Angel Maker, or if it was all in my head. If I was connecting dots where there shouldn't be connections. It wouldn't be the first time I'd overreacted.

Callie's feet shuffled from the hallway, and I heard her reach into the fridge for something. Within a minute, she popped around the couch and saw my crumbled form. "Tonight I'm staying in," she said, immediately groaning and gripping the side of her head. In her other hand, she had a bottle of water and some pain-relievers. "You want to do a movie night, like we used to do in middle school?"

I wasn't sure why she wanted to have a throwback to our childhoods, but I nodded against the pillow, which seemed to appease her. I was too tired to go to Edward's and Lincoln's tonight anyway, and if they asked, this would be the perfect excuse.

Besides, it'd been ages since Callie wanted to have a night in with me.

I couldn't let myself sleep the whole day away, so after a little more laziness, I got up and showered. Callie was in her room, probably sleeping off her hangover, which meant I had a few hours of quiet in the house. A few hours of silence were all I needed to whip up my next blog post.

This next one, I decided, would be a call-out post. I would know soon enough whether or not the Angel Maker was focused on me.

After I showered and changed, I grabbed my laptop and got to it. My fingers typed furiously; writing about him, practically writing to him, and it was easier than I thought it would be. The words flowed out of me at an impressive rate, and before Callie got up, my next blog post was done. Proofed and everything.

I read over it one last time before publishing it, and I followed the comments all day, until Callie got up.

I let her choose the movies and pick the food. Pizza. She wanted pizza. While I fiddled with the oven to put one of those frozen pizzas inside, she put in the first movie. We were going to have a Disney marathon, I guess. Disney was something everyone seemed to like, and while I enjoyed the animation, I could never really get into them. Something about the good guys always winning seemed…fake.

Because the truth was, the good guys didn't always win. In real life, the good guys lost just as much as the bad guys did. The bad guys did whatever they had to to win, which was something I'd always respected. While the heroes had lines they wouldn't cross, the villains didn't.

The villains were my kind of characters, and in Disney movies, they always lost.

I needed a movie where the villain won. I needed to see something where the heroes fought valiantly yet still lost in a bloody, gory display. I needed more than these children's movies could offer.

But it was fine. I didn't focus on the movies, and neither did Callie, unless it was one of the movie's many musical numbers, of which she had to sing along while giggling. We spent most of the afternoon and night talking like we used to. She asked me question after question about Edward and Lincoln, still shocked I'd gone over to their house *again*.

Of course, I didn't tell her how I'd wound up at their house, just that Lincoln and Edward wanted to see me. It wasn't like Callie would ever understand how I'd felt when Lincoln announced he'd been there to kill me. It had been…an indescribable feeling, one any sane person would never comprehend.

"So," Callie started, shoving a piece of cold pizza into her mouth, "does that mean you're like a thruple now?"

I blinked at her. "A thruple?"

"Yeah, you know. A couple, but with three people instead of two."

Thinking on this, I slowly said, "I haven't seen Lincoln and Edward together like that, if that's what you mean." If they were only with me and not with each other, what did that make us? I wasn't even sure putting a label on it was a good thing to do, considering we'd never talked about what we were yet.

Edward had talked to me during the drive home, though, about Killian. He didn't want me to see him again, in any non-professional capacity. No more dates with my boss. I could handle it, since it wasn't like I wanted to date Killian anyways. I wasn't even sure why I'd said yes to begin with. Killian…I wasn't into guys like him. Too preppy. Too normal. Too…everyday and average.

Callie let out a laugh. "Then you're just the meat in the man sandwich? God, Stella, I'm so jealous of you. Don't tell John I said that."

"I won't," I said, trying to smile. I never had even met John, so it was very unlikely I'd ever talk to him about anything Callie said. "When is John coming back to town?" I didn't know much about him, only that he worked as a businessman or something for some company that required a lot of travel. He seemed to be out of town more than he was in it. Had to be difficult on their relationship, right?

"I'm not sure. From what it sounds like, the deal isn't going too well," Callie spoke, checking her phone to see if John had texted her. He didn't, so she quickly put it down. "I was hoping he'd be home by Monday, but now it might not be till Friday." She groaned. "Long distance is hard, but the money's good."

Money. Money was something Callie's family didn't really have to worry about. They were loaded.

Time passed in a blur. The world turned to night, and all was quiet on the Edward and Lincoln front. I wondered what they were doing, wondering if they would not see other women since Edward clearly didn't want me to see any other guy. It was only fair, right? If we were...committed to each other, there would be no one else for any of us. Strangely, though, the thought didn't worry me too much. Somehow I knew they cared for me in a vastly different way than any of the others they'd brought home.

I put in the next movie and went back to the couch, getting under the blanket we were sharing and tucking my legs beneath my butt. My toes grazed Callie's leg, and even under the blanket, she was cold.

I asked, "Do you want me to get you another blanket? You're freezing."

Callie shrugged. "Nah, I'm fine. I always run cold. You know that."

Nodding, I knew it was true. It was something I'd gotten used to over the years.

Both of our attention went to the TV screen across from us. Callie was oblivious to the fact that Lincoln and I had had sex on the floor right in front of where we sat on the couch. I must've done a better job than I thought at cleaning it all up, because there was a lot of bodily fluids involved. Lincoln was…very good with his tongue and his fingers, when he wasn't using them to insult me or try to kill me.

It hadn't escaped my notice that Lincoln was gentler last night than he'd ever been. Whether or not it meant he finally realized I belonged with them was up for debate. Lincoln seemed a stubborn sort, so I bet he'd need more convincing. Honestly, though, I wasn't sure what else I could do to convince him. I'd found a dead girl in his bed and hadn't run from him, screaming. He'd tried to kill me, and I'd slept with him half a dozen times.

I mean, what more could I do? What more was there to do? Maybe he just needed time. He had to be used to his life with just him and Edward. He had to be a creature of habit. My sudden appearance in his life had been unwelcome; I knew Edward was the one who followed my articles, not him. Lincoln had no reason to be as obsessed with me like Edward was.

Time. I would give him time. How much time? I couldn't say, but I'd try to be patient, because I couldn't give either of them up. A thruple, whatever the hell we would be—I wanted it. I wanted to be with them.

I wanted them more than anything, more than life itself.

Chapter Twenty-Five - The Angel Maker

I know it isn't my usual posting time, but I find I cannot keep my thoughts to myself. I know you're all used to my rambling thoughts—I let my blog posts run rampant sometimes, freer with my words here than I ever am with the articles I publish with the Tribune—but this post is...it's going to be different than the others.

Because, while I normally ramble away my thoughts or give you little known facts about history's many serial killers, today's post won't deal with that. This is unlike any other post I've ever done.

It's a call-out post. This post is meant for only one person's eyes, even though I know more than one set will see it. My blog has been and will always be public, and maybe that's why my reach is so wide. You are used to me telling you the truth in my Tribune articles if you follow me there, so I'm going to be blunt.

This is for you. You know who you are. There isn't a doubt in your mind that this isn't for you—which is good, because I would never expect someone like you to have self-doubts. How could you, with everything you've done and everything you still plan on doing?

We both know you're not finished yet. We both know there will be more to come. More death, more blood, more questions. Let's not pretend otherwise, you and I. We're both smarter than that.

Let's get down to the nitty and gritty then: this article is for you, simply because I want to ask you some questions. Why them? Did their lives matter to you, or were they just in the wrong place at the wrong time? Though I suppose it would be the opposite for you—they were in the right place at the right time to become one of your victims. But I digress.

Why do they pray? Is it salvation they seek, even after death? Or is it you they are praying to—their god of blood and death, their savior from the chaos of the world? After all, what could God give them that you couldn't?

How long have you planned this? How many years did these ideas stew in your head, formulating in your mind until you had something concrete? Have you killed before? I bet you have. I bet murder is nothing new to you...which begs another question.

Why do this now? What was it about this week that made you decide it was the week to unleash yourself upon the world, a scourge upon mankind? Tell me, because I am dying to know.

The truth is I want to know more about you. I need to know more. If you're reading this, which I have a strong feeling you are, tell me more. I want to know more about you, what made you, what thoughts run through your head as you slice up your victims and arrange their hands toward the sky.

Why make them pray when they're already dead? What purpose does it have?

Are you a religious man? Do you believe in God? In an afterlife? Pray tell, I want to know everything there is to know about you, because I can't help but feel like I brought you here. Not that I made you, per se; not like I crafted you out of stone and set you loose upon the world. But I had a hand in this, as did every other person who loves to read about you.

We made you. We created you. Society has failed you, and now you want to make it pay and have us watch and wonder. But I am not scared of you, unlike the others. I am not afraid of you or what you could do.

Now this is when you might be asking your own questions. Why am I unafraid? Why am I not frightened of you like the rest of the populace? After all, you could theoretically strike at any moment. You could be anyone, wear any face, and no one would know. How am I so bold that I could freely tell you I am not scared?

Because I am not. Because like you, I am different than everyone else. Because I am curious and I am logical. There is nothing to fear in this life. Nothing at all. Fear is a man-made construction. Fear is not real.

I am not afraid of you, and if I ever met you, I would say it to your face. You might think you hold the power, you may think you are unstoppable, but you are just a man. Deep down, you aren't so different from me. We are alike in more ways than you think.

Tell me more about you. About where you came from. Tell me everything about you, and I promise you I'll do you justice in ways the news stations would never, could never. I won't psychoanalyze you; only say what is. What will be. I would give you the respect you deserve, because you are a cut above the rest. You are just a man, but you are so much more.

You are more than your skin and your bones put together. You are your mind, and I am dying to delve into it and feel the things you feel.

By now, even if you aren't who I'm talking you, you've probably already guessed who this particular blog post is for. You might even be thinking of commenting and pretending to be him. In which case, I'll know you're not, because the person I'm talking to would never do something so asinine, so leave it be, and let him come to me without your interference.

Yes, this is all for you, Angel Maker. I want answers.

I'll be waiting for your next reveal with bated breath. Don't keep me waiting too long.

I couldn't believe she'd be so bold as to write an entire blog post dedicated to me. Almost like it was meant for my eyes only. So she knew I did this all for her. She knew, and yet she was still so blind. It never ceased to amaze me how blind people were.

Until I made them see. Until I took them and forced them to their knees, made them pray to whatever God they might've believed in. Did their God ever answer?

No, because there was no God. There was no ultimate being in the sky who could save them from their pain. There was nothing up there that could save them from me.

It wasn't like I thought I was some all-powerful being. Just like she'd said, I was but a man. However, I was a man who knew what I was capable of. Everyone else never lived up to their potential. I was helping them.

That seemed to not be something she understood.

She claimed to be like me, almost claimed to know me, and yet she was so oblivious to everything I did. She did not know me. I'd realized recently if I wanted to get her attention, it would have to be something big.

What bigger way than calling out to her inner animal? What bigger way than exciting the beast dwelling within her? If she was like me, she needed a wakeup call. Stella Wilson would get one, and I hoped it would be what she wanted.

She wanted blood? She wanted death and destruction? Then she'd get it.

I was so fucking tired of being unseen. So over the whole invisible to everyone else thing. I wanted everyone to see me as who I was, not who I pretended to be. I wanted to step into the limelight—and I wanted her to be with me.

She should be with me. I would make her see the light, see the truth of the matter. She was mine, she just didn't know it.

I thought it ironic she published this post today. Ironic because I had another person, ready to go. She was still alive, but she wouldn't be for long. I had a place set up, and prior to this, I actually had a plan that involved Stella. Everything would have to move up on my timeline, but I could make it work. I had to.

How many times had she seen me? How many times had we been in the same fucking place, and she had no idea who she was looking at? I was tired of being a stranger in my own skin. This was not the life I wanted to live. I needed change, and tonight I would get it. Soon enough, she would see.

Tonight, everything would change.

Tonight, Stella would realize that she'd always been mine.

Chapter Twenty-Six - Stella

Callie and I went to bed around two in the morning. Late, considering what we'd both been up to the night before. I dragged her to bed before plopping down in my own, too tired to crawl beneath the sheets and get cuddly. I just wanted the sweet release of dreamless sleep.

And I almost had it too. I dozed off for fifteen minutes before I heard something in the front of the house.

Did Callie get up? She had no alcohol tonight, so there was no way she was drunk, but I had to make sure she didn't try baking chocolate chip cookies at five hundred degrees again. Yeah, our first month of renting this house had been super fun, since Callie was still stuck in the partying mindset of her college days.

Just to be safe—because I didn't feel like paying for damages to our landlord again—I got myself out of bed and shuffled down the hall. I peeked through the crack of Callie's door, finding she was still asleep in her bed.

Hmm. Maybe I hadn't heard anything after all.

Still, just to be safe, I carried onward to check it out. My feet drew me into the living room, where I immediately saw something wasn't right. Namely the front door. It hung wide open, inviting any stranger inside wordlessly.

My brows went together, and as I went to close it, I couldn't help but think something was wrong. I knew the door had been closed when we went to bed not fifteen minutes ago, and doors didn't just open on their own. They always needed someone's help, especially when they were locked.

Hand flat against the door, I was second from fully shutting it when an arm snaked around my neck, pressing tightly against my throat, ripping me away from the door. An intruder, and it was too late for me to fight back. I hadn't seen him, and now that I knew he was here, it was too late. He had me in a compromising position instantly.

Stronger than me, taller than me too—though nowhere near as tall as Edward and Lincoln, so I knew it wasn't them. I knew Lincoln hadn't changed his mind about me. This was someone else.

My breath caught in my throat, partly because I was being restrained with an arm that lifted me off my feet and didn't let me breathe, and partly because I was shocked. Stunned. Surprised.

Was this man the Angel Maker? Was he here for me? My article had to have done this.

Wait. What about Callie?

If I had anything to compare Lincoln's loyalty to Edward to, it was mine to Callie. Callie didn't deserve to die at the hands of the Angel Maker. She was meant for so much more. She was my only friend.

So I fought.

I fought and I struggled and I kicked out my legs, but I couldn't touch him, couldn't get his arm away from my neck. My vision started to blur, and before I knew what was happening, unconsciousness took over, pulling me into a painful, blackened sleep.

I couldn't say whether I was alive or dead, and I couldn't tell how much time had passed. I did know it was still dark when I slowly regained consciousness, struggling to open my eyes. My lids felt like stone, and my body felt weak, tired. What being strangled would do to you, apparently.

Something hard and rough sat beneath me, cold. The wind blew against my back, alerting me to the fact I was outside somewhere, maybe on concrete. Based on the temperature against my skin, I'd say it was still nighttime, which would mean I didn't lose much time. Still—any amount of time lost was too much.

Callie.

My hands were unbound, as were my legs, and I struggled to get up, to open my eyes. My whole body didn't want to listen. It wanted to fall over and sleep the night away. Every time I swallowed, my throat was bruised, and I would bet anything my voice would be raspy.

I had one thing on my mind: Callie. I had to make sure she was okay, had to make sure he didn't go after her, too. What would I do if I lost Callie? If I woke up and found my one and only friend dead in front of me? Would my mind even survive something like that? I would never be whole again, not that I was too whole as I was right now. I might've been broken, I might've been weird, but at least I wasn't alone.

When I sat up and opened my eyes, I found I was alone, in the middle of a department store parking lot, with nothing but the moon shining above me. I got to my feet, staring at the distance between me and the department store's doors. A hundred feet, maybe.

It was a surreal thing, being in a gigantic parking lot so late, with no cars near me. My body felt like iron, my knees not wanting to cooperate. It was almost like I wasn't inside my own body, like I watched from afar, as this thing happened to someone else.

If that was the Angel Maker, why was I still alive? Why was I here, alone? What pieces of the puzzle wasn't I seeing?

Then the wind caressed my back, and almost on cue, lights flashed on behind me, powered by tiny generators. So bright, before I turned around, I knew what they were: spotlights. Meaning, of course, I wasn't alone. Meaning there was something behind me he wanted me to see.

I felt my eyes grow teary. It couldn't be Callie. It wouldn't be. It had to be someone else.

Repeating this mantra to myself, I slowly turned around. I felt almost naked in my shorts and my loose shirt, my nighttime clothes. My pajamas. My hair was wild and down, whipping in my face with the wind when I turned, tendrils getting into my mouth. But I didn't pull them out, because I was too awe-struck at the scene before me.

The first thing my mind thought: *it's not Callie*. The second thing: *it's someone else I know*.

Standing before me with her hands held together was Sandy. Her body was free of all clothing, allowing me to see the wrinkles and the cellulite that came along with middle age. Her hands were tied together by a stained zip tie, her fingers pointing toward the sky. Her head was bent back, her mouth hanging open slightly.

Her eyes were open and glassy, glazed over with an expression only a dead woman would wear. With the spotlights beside her, I could see the flies buzzing around her, but she didn't smell yet.

Meaning she was fresh.

Sandy was held up, kept standing by makeshift poles jutting through her flesh. Two through her knees, one impaling her chest. All of them leaned against the concrete parking lot below, keeping her upright. Keeping her praying. Her back was eerily black, almost like no lights were shining there purposefully.

I also didn't see any blood on her body, which meant the Angel Maker was adapting, becoming cleaner in his kills. The only bits of blood I saw were around the poles sticking out of her skin, and even that was hardly enough to note. Sandy had been dead long before the poles were stuck through her body, her heart already stopped. Once the heart was stopped, you didn't bleed nearly as much, because there was nothing pumping it.

I took a step closer to her and I gazed up at her frozen face. I wasn't a huge fan of Sandy, but it wasn't like I wanted her dead. She could take Killian off my hands. I had Edward and Lincoln now. She…she didn't show up to work Thursday or Friday. We all had thought it was weird, because she never took off, even when massively hung over or sick.

Here she'd been caught by the Angel Maker, held captive until her body could be useful.

I knew if she was killed Friday or even Thursday night, there would be a much more rancid taste in the air, more coppery. This was fresh. This had happened today…because of my article?

Was this the Angel Maker's answer to my questions?

I was drawn to her body, like a moth to the flame. I didn't look around me, didn't hear the sirens wailing in the distance. I took another step nearer. I must've tripped something, a tiny, thin wire so small the eyes could not see, for suddenly Sandy's body jerked forward.

Or, should I say, her back jerked.

New lights flashed on, lights situated behind her, illuminating a piece of the puzzle I couldn't see in the darkness before.

I stumbled, falling to my knees before her. She was...she was beautiful. I'd never seen anything like her before. She was so perfect she hurt my eyes, the blindingly bright spotlights aside.

Sandy wasn't just held up by poles inside her body. She wasn't only praying to the sky, caught in a wide-eyed expression. Her back was cut, her skin carefully sawed-off and attached to thin wires. Two poles stood behind her body, not impaling her, but peeling her back skin off and holding it there.

Thin, flimsy flesh, I could see through the layer that was carved off, though parts of it looked like they were still attached to her back at the base...almost like wings. Like gory, fleshy wings made of the stuff of nightmares. I knew her back was a red mess, having its skin shorn off like that. Peeled off like a banana, only redder and bloodier, held apart by the poles and thin wires.

Sandy was a true angel. Sandy had met the end the others should have.

This was what the Angel Maker was about. This is what he wanted everyone to see.

And he wanted me to be the first one to see it.

The sirens were coming closer, and still I could not move myself away from the body. I knelt less than five feet from her, and yet I felt worlds below her, worlds less than her. How could I ever amount to such perfection?

This was…it was a memory that would be burned into my head, vivid and bright, assailing and violent, until the day I died. I would never forget this. I would dream of this, even though I'd never dreamt before.

Multiple police cars turned into the large parking lot, circling around Sandy and I, their lights assaulting my senses, their sirens just a bit too loud. They gave me a headache. I could barely hear them as they got out of their cars, cracked open their doors and pointed their guns at me, telling me to slowly raise my hands, place them on the back of my head and lay on my stomach.

Did they believe me to be the culprit? Did they think I was the one who killed Sandy and fashioned her into an angel with her very own wings of flesh?

An ambulance was on its way too, and though Sandy demanded my attention, I had enough of myself to realize it I had to listen to the police's orders or get shot, possibly killed. I let out a sigh as I sluggishly lifted my hands and wove my fingers together, placing them on the back of my head.

If only Lincoln was a cop in this town. He wouldn't shoot me. Maybe he'd let me stare at her for a while longer…

I got onto my stomach, my head bent at an almost unnatural angle so I could keep watch over Sandy. This was more than I'd asked for with my blog post. This was simultaneously too much and not enough at all. Now that I had a taste for what the Angel Maker could do, it wasn't enough. This wasn't nearly enough.

I needed more.

I lost myself in a daze as one of the cops came to me, setting a knee on my back as he cuffed my hands. I could hardly feel her, or him, or whatever he was, because I was so intently focused on Sandy and her glorious fleshy wings.

The cop dragged me to my feet, taking me to the backseat of his car while the other cops were measured in moving closer to Sandy. Some of them looked like they were going to be sick; others held a frown on their faces, as if they were disgusted at the violence, at the death. I couldn't understand them—why weren't they as amazed at her as I was? Why couldn't they see how flawless she was?

Sandy was the Angel Maker's first true victim. The others had been for show, to get my attention. Sandy was the first…and I'd been here to see it.

I felt my lips curling into a grin as the cop slammed the door in my face. He didn't read me my rights, so I wasn't sure whether I was getting arrested or not. I didn't care. My forehead was glued to the window, my eyes lingering on Sandy's body, at her pale, fleshy wings.

This was the start of a new chapter.

This was only the beginning.

Chapter Twenty-Seven - Lincoln

Ed had surprised me earlier, when he'd told me his plan, and I would be the first one to admit, I still wasn't certain whether Stella should be included in our little duo. But she was an odd one, and there was something about her that drew me in, just like she drew Ed in. She was our brand of crazy…I just wasn't sure if her crazy would jive permanently with ours.

Inviting someone into our lives, a permanent position at our sides, it wasn't an easy or a simple thing. It wasn't like we went around telling everyone *Come on over, come join the fun. There's orgies, good food, and murder. What's not to like?*

Yeah, we might attract the wrong crowd with a line like that.

Ed had called me during his first break with an idea I was hesitant of. He was so gung-ho about Stella, and after last night, I supposed it was pointless of me to deny the fact I felt something for her, too.

I could promise you, the number of times I went to kill someone and didn't actually kill them…well, I could count them on one hand. One single finger. Stella was just fucking special like that, I guess.

I would not be the one to tell Ed no, not again—not so soon after my attempted murder of Stella, anyways—so I told him I would take care of it. By the time he got home, I would have it all ready to go, and the only part we'd be missing would be Stella herself.

After this…we'd really know whether or not she was one of us. We'd know beyond a shadow of a doubt whether she was meant to be with us or just someone we had over for fun.

I drove through the bad parts of town, knowing exactly where they were because I was often called over there when shootings happened, when there were overdoses. Because of my frequenting of the area, I knew where there were cameras, and which street corners to pass by in search of someone who piqued my interest.

Luckily for Ed, and unluckily for her, I had someone in mind already. Someone who'd been into the station on prostitution charges more than once, and drug charges quite a few times in between. Her pimp always had the money to get her out, and she never narked on him, never snitched.

Oh, yes. Destiny would meet her destiny tonight. Or maybe tomorrow. Whenever the hell Ed decided to get Stella back to our house and show her the basement.

The basement was not an area of our house that we let anyone into, unless they were going to meet their death soon after. Our basement was our secret place, with chains and sterile walls, a constant smell of bleach. It was also soundproof; we'd made sure of that. It was our, for lack of a better word, playroom. Where Ed and I unleashed our inner psychos.

Stella thought I was mad for strangling a girl in my bed? She thought Ed was a little rough during sex? She had no idea what cruelty we were both capable of. With hearts as cruel and as black as ours, there was no limit to what we could do. To what we would do.

The night was dark as I pulled up to the street corner where I saw two women standing, wearing the littlest, flimsiest clothing they could while still covering all the important bits. They were two gorgeous women, with curves and tits to match. A redhead and a blonde. It was the blonde that caught my eye.

Unfortunately, it was the redhead who approached my open window, leaning down with a supple smile on her face. She checked me out, probably wondering what a guy like me was doing here. Couldn't I get laid like any other handsome guy? I'd seen her before, but she was never brought into the station.

And I looked very different out of my uniform, so I didn't blame her for not recognizing me.

"Hey there, baby. What's on the menu for tonight?" the redhead asked, pressing her arms closer to her tits, making her breasts pop out more. They were nice, but not what I was here for.

I gave her a charming smile—something I loathed doing. I wasn't the charming one. Ed was. "I was actually hoping to get Destiny tonight. Tell her I'll pay double her usual rate." My wallet sat in my car's cup holder, and I reached inside and pulled out a fifty, handing it to her once I noticed her pouting, annoying face. "For getting your hopes up."

She took the money and sauntered off, shouting for Destiny.

Destiny didn't even look before she got in the car. She adjusted her skirt, showing the strings on her thong, before she even looked at me. By the time her eyes met mine, I'd already driven down the road and locked the door.

"You…" She sputtered, recognition dawning on her face. It would've been pretty, if it wasn't caked in so much makeup you couldn't tell what she looked like underneath. I'd seen her mugshot. I knew what she looked like under all that powder. Not half bad. "What the hell, I didn't—"

I gave her a smile. "I'm not arresting you tonight, Destiny."

She relaxed a little. "Oh." She studied me. "You really came to pick me up for…" For a woman who worked as a prostitute, she was remarkably good at playing coy. Too bad I wasn't in the mood for coy. I wasn't in the mood for a lot, considering there was a half-dressed woman in my car who I was fairly certain was beyond skilled with her tongue.

"I'm having a party, and the guys voted on the entertainment." I shot her a look. "Don't worry, Destiny. I'll pay fair for each of them."

Destiny was slow to smirk. "Don't tell me your party involves other boys in blue. I'm not sure if my poor little heart can handle all that."

"The only cop who'll be there is me," I said. "And I'm not on duty." My eyes flicked to her as I drove to the house. She'd come with me for the money. Normally they didn't go too far from their turf, and they had a chosen motel where most of their business occurred. Still, I felt she was hesitant. "I've always wondered how good you are with that mouth." Flirting wasn't one of the things I was best at, but I had found most women take a shine to a man who wasn't afraid to say what he wanted, to say the truth.

Though, Destiny wasn't getting the entire truth, and by the time she realized it, it would be too late. There would be no running for her. No escaping from the fate Ed and I had planned for her.

Destiny let out a half grin. "Somehow that don't surprise me none. I always knew there was something off about you. I just didn't know what."

The rest of the ride, she was amused to herself, and I let her think I couldn't get women on my own. The truth was I could get anyone I wanted, man, woman, or not. I could take them, and they wouldn't be able to fight me. I was too strong for most people, too intimidating for others.

To say I was just like everyone else would do a disservice to me, because I was so much more. I was a beast, an animal, and sometimes killing did not sate me. Sometimes I needed more. Until now, Ed was the only other person who truly knew me for me, who knew who and what I was behind the mask I wore in my everyday life.

Would Stella become the second person to do so? Would she want to? Would she go along with this willingly, or had Ed vastly overestimated her craziness? I'd admit, I didn't think she'd tell us no, because I didn't believe Stella was the type of woman who looked away from the blood and the gore.

No, she was the kind of person who stared at things head on. The kind of person to look the bull in the eyes before getting the horns. Soon enough we'd find out whether she wasn't crazy enough for us, or if she was just right.

As I pulled into our driveway and into our garage, Destiny made a big show about looking around. "I didn't see many cars on the street," she said, probably because we didn't live in a cozy residential community. We lived on a street where people loved to speed by, never paying any attention to the houses on it.

I turned off the car and hit the button on the opener to close the garage door. "Can't have my neighbors thinking I'm some party animal," I said. At least Ed's car was already here, meaning he was somewhere inside the house. Not that I thought this woman would get the better of me, but just in case.

You couldn't be too careful. Sometimes people surprised you.

Sometimes they didn't.

Destiny nodded along, as if my flimsy excuse made sense. About as much sense as her outfit, which was garish and ugly and ridiculously revealing. A tiny skirt which showed most of her ass, along with a tube top that looked vastly uncomfortable. Honestly, I wasn't even sure how she fit her tits into it.

I waited for her to walk around the car in her dollar store high heels, grabbing her hand as I led her into the house. She spotted an empty living room and kitchen, immediately saying, "Where the hell is the party? What—"

It was all she had the chance to say, before I turned on her and gave her a chilling smile. This smile was more akin to how I felt inside. This particular smile was one hundred percent dead inside, and she knew it, for her confused expression twisted into one of fear, and she muttered a string of swearwords as she tried to yank her hand from mine.

She was nowhere near strong enough to escape my grip, which she soon realized as I started dragging her through the kitchen, to the door attached to the stairwell. With her free hand, she reached to her side, pulling out a tiny, pink can of pepper spray. Before she could shoot any of it at me, I grabbed her wrist, slamming her against the wall of the stairs. My thumb increased pressure on her wrist until I nearly broke it, and the bitch held onto the pink plastic can until the very last second.

"Fuck," she whimpered, dropping the spray to the floor. "I knew you were fucked up. I knew it from the first moment I laid eyes on you—"

I gave her an unimpressed look before releasing the hand that had very nearly sprayed me, backhanding her across the face. I didn't even blink as I did it, but Destiny…oh, she felt it, and her skin was red instantly. I flung open the basement door and tugged her along.

She wailed, cried, shouted. She struggled and tried to pull away from me, but I had her other arm still, and no one ran from me. Especially not this one. The streets wouldn't miss her, and neither would my precinct.

The moment we emerged from the stairs and Destiny saw our basement in its full glory, she froze. "What the fuck?" she whispered, and I only smirked as I brought her to the wall where the chains hung, meeting her questioning eyes as I locked her up. Wrists and ankles.

Once she was restrained fully, I took a step back, studying my handiwork. She looked good, chained to the wall, even with her makeup running with the tears forming in the corners of her eyes. My dick ached in my pants when I thought about Stella cutting into her. She'd have to enjoy it.

Before leaving Destiny in the darkness, I said, "I look forward to watching you bleed, bitch." When she started wailing, when she began to shake the chains and rattle them against the wall, I spun and left the basement, closing the door behind me, blocking out her cries.

I bent to pick up her tiny can of pepper spray the exact same moment Ed came down the stairs, running a towel over his head. He wore only pants, its button and zipper undone. "You got her?" he asked.

I nodded, swinging her pink can of pepper spray around my pointer finger. "Yep. The bitch almost pepper sprayed me."

"But she didn't." Ed inhaled a giant sigh. "And now we have her. All that's left is to get Stella over here." The hand moving the towel over his hair dropped to his side as he thought. "Let's give her tonight. Tomorrow, her whole world will change." His blue eyes flicked downward, noting the bulge in my pants. "You might want to take care of that, though."

I wanted to punch him. Obviously I had to take care of it, and since Stella wasn't here to relieve me—and the bitch downstairs was off limits—my hand it was. My fucking hand was nowhere near as fun as making someone else do it, but after tonight, hopefully it would be the last time. With any luck, Stella would be around to take care of these things for me in the future.

Because that bitch in the basement? Destiny wasn't going to be our kill; she was to be Stella's.

Chapter Twenty-Eight – Stella

They kept me alone for a long time, chained to a table. I wasn't in jail, not in a cell, but I might as well have been. The room was boring and plain, white and blue, save for the one-way mirror on the wall and the tiny camera in the room's upper corner. I stared into the camera, at its flashing red light, wondering what those watching me saw.

Did they think I was the culprit? Did they believe me to be the Angel Maker? Preposterous, and stupid. I wasn't nearly as muscular enough as one would have to be to impale someone with pipes and lug their body into a parking lot without struggling and getting caught. No, if these cops thought I was their suspect, they had another thing coming.

I wasn't the Angel Maker. I couldn't be. And while they kept me in here, it was very probable that he was out there, continuing his spree.

Of course, now that I thought about it, it was official. Eastland county had its own serial killer. We had our own, and he was mine.

I wasn't claiming to have made him, but I dubbed him the Angel Maker. I wrote to him in my blog and he came to me that same night. We had a special relationship, me and him. I just had no idea who he was or why I was so important to him.

Important. I had to be important to him, otherwise why would he have let me keep my life? What was another life to a grand serial killer? I should've meant nothing to him, and yet I clearly meant more.

These cops…I hoped they wouldn't keep me here forever, because I had someone to meet, a trail to follow. I needed to know who the Angel Maker was, not to turn him into the authorities, but to just know.

I had to know.

I had to know, because I felt some strange kinship to him. Granted, I'd never cut off someone's skin and peeled off wings from their back, but we were alike in so many other ways. The outcasts of society. The people who no one looked at twice.

Let's be serious here. If I didn't have heterochromia, no one would look at me. No one would notice me. I would fly under everyone's radar. I wasn't drop-dead gorgeous. I wasn't unique in any way, other than my eyes. I felt as ostracized from society as the Angel Maker did. We were more alike than he knew.

Or maybe he did know. Maybe he knew we were the same, and that's why he was doing all of this for me.

Because it was for me. I knew it was all for me. These people—Sandy—they were all dead for me, and instead of shocked and horrified, I was grateful. I no longer felt dead inside, and I owed it to the Angel Maker.

I would get out of here, and I would meet him.

I would thank him.

Chapter Twenty-Nine - Killian

This wasn't how I thought it would go. This wasn't at all like how I planned our weekend to be. If Stella hadn't run away from me, everything could've gone according to plan. But no—here I was, in the early hours of dawn, parking my car a few houses down from hers, getting out with a scowl on my face.

I had leather gloves on, and they itched as I headed to the sidewalk and walked up her driveway. After tossing a look behind me to make sure no one was out and watching, I reached into my pocket and pulled out my kit. I was inside the front door within a minute, closing it behind me.

The house was not hers. It was rented, the same house she'd been in for the last few years, ever since she graduated from college and moved here with her friend. Callie.

After waiting a moment and not hearing anything, I started to investigate my dear Stella. I found a mess in the living room, a plate of half-eaten pizza and a single can of pop. A blanket hung over the couch, used. I ran my leather-clad hand over it, slowly curling my fingers around it and bringing it to my face, inhaling.

Like lavender. Like Stella. A calming, soothing scent.

I set the blanket down, moving to the hall. It seemed no one was home, which was a good thing, because right now I needed time to think. I knew Stella had gone home with that blonde from the bar. Deep down, in my gut, I knew it and I hated it.

So I did a little stalking. It was something I was remarkably good at.

Imagine my surprise when I discovered she was with not only one man but two. Two guys, yet she couldn't even look at me for longer than a minute without disgust crossing her face. Those guys didn't know who she was. They didn't know her like I did. I'd known her for years now. I'd broken up with Julie for *her*. I ended things for us, because I knew Stella was supposed to be *mine*.

I would not give her up to two strangers.

I took a quick peek into the bathroom, staring at myself in the mirror before opening the medicine cabinet and looking inside the drawers of the vanity. I left everything how I found it, and I was about to close the last drawer when something round and orange caught my eye. Hesitant, I lifted it from the drawer, spinning it to see the prescription name and the date it was given.

It was a year old, and still full.

I didn't recognize the name of the medication, but I filed it away in my head as I returned the pill container to the drawer and slowly closed it.

Stella's room was right next door to the bathroom, and I went straight there, surveying the space. Not a huge room, but full to the brim with her smell. Her clothes and her belongings. I'd never felt closer to her than I did right now, when I stood in her room, unknown to her. This was where she slept, when she wasn't caught up in those two assholes.

This was where I would make Stella mine.

Because she would be mine; she just didn't know it yet.

I spent the next few minutes searching her room. I wasn't sure what I'd find. Maybe I wasn't searching for anything. Maybe all I wanted was for her to walk through the door, see me, and realize what she'd been missing. I wanted her to grasp her mistake and do her best to remedy it, to fix it. I wanted her to come to me, lead me to the bed and get to know me in a way we'd never gotten to know each other before.

I had been the world's biggest idiot for letting Sandy take me to the bathroom. For letting her yank down my pants and put her mouth around me. I had been weak, but I swore to myself I'd never be weak again. I would be strong, for Stella.

Everything was for Stella.

In a few minutes, I left Stella's room, moving across the hall to Callie's. In all the time I'd known her, I'd only ever seen her text her. I'd never actually seen Callie, even when I tried to get Stella to bring her to the Christmas party last year. If Callie was such a huge aspect of her life, I wanted to know about it. I needed to know everything there was to know about Stella, and Callie would've been the easiest way.

But maybe it was better this way. I liked a challenge just as much as the next guy; it would only make my victory that much sweeter.

When I stepped into Callie's room, I spotted a made-up bed. Nothing was out of place in her room. It was all so…clean and orderly. Which, judging from Stella's stories of her, was not what I'd been expecting.

A desk sat along the wall, and I turned to study it, noticing the laptop sitting atop it, plugged in and fully charged, by the look of it. A phone rested on top of the laptop, also plugged in and fully charged if its little green light meant anything.

Something was wrong here.

If Callie's phone was here, where was Callie?

I hit the phone screen, and the screen lit up, showing me dozens of missed calls and over a hundred text messages, from various people. From someone named John, from someone labeled Mom, and even some from Stella.

This...this wasn't right. No one left their phone anywhere nowadays, let alone let so many texts and calls go unanswered.

I ran a finger across the desk's wood, slowly realizing the entire thing—laptop included—was covered in a thick layer of dust, as if it hadn't been touched in months.

Odd.

Rubbing my fingers together, I studied the room in a new light. This entire room was like someone cleaned up and then forgot about it, never stepping foot in it again. Even the air inside was stale.

I stepped near the window, about to lift it open, but my eyes saw something weird as I gaze out into the backyard. A simple square of green grass, surrounded by a wooden fence...except for the lone flower bed directly outside of the window. Completely out of place, as if someone had put it there as an afterthought.

My energy was renewed as I left Callie's room, returning to the bathroom, taking in things I didn't see before. Things my eyes glazed over my first trip here.

One toothbrush. One shampoo in the shower. One towel on the towel rack.

Just…*one* of everything.

Suddenly, I knew.

I went through the house, moving to the door that led to the attached garage. I flipped on the light, illuminating the dark space. A spick-and-span garage with no car inside. Gardening tools were arranged on the walls, and I moved before the tool I needed. In my gut, I already knew, but I had to be sure.

Stella was definitely throwing me for a curveball here.

After grabbing the shovel, I exited through the garage's side man door, and I headed around to the backyard, stopping only when I stood before the flowerbed. I stared at it for too long, let my mind wander too much before I got to work. The flowers were strong and healthy, their stalks thick and sturdy. This flowerbed had been here for at least this season.

I started digging.

It was early enough in the day no one else was outside, before the sun rose in the sky and started to warm the world. I had peace and quiet as I tore through the flower bed. It was about a foot and a half down, and I knew it the moment the tip of the shovel hit something hard. The sound of metal crunching through skin and bone bounced in the air, and I immediately dropped the shovel and fell to my knees, reaching into the hole, flicking away the dirt until I saw it.

Or, maybe I should say, until I saw *her*.

Until I saw a rotting neck, flesh that had not seen the light of day for a while.

Callie.

My heart nearly stopped. I didn't think...I mean, not once did I ever suspect Stella of being capable of something like this. Really, it wasn't a wonder why I was so drawn to her from the beginning.

God, I fucking loved that woman, and I'd do anything to make her realize she loved me too.

As I began to return to the dirt to its hole, the sound of a car door slamming caught my attention. My back went rod straight. Odd. I could've sworn it came from the front of the house, which was impossible, because no one was here. At least, no one should be here for quite a while, not that I knew Callie was six feet under, metaphorically speaking.

More like two feet, but still.

I gripped the shovel tightly, moving slowly around the house. There was a car parked in the driveway, and with a sinking heart, I knew whoever it was was already inside the house. I went in through the side of the garage, still gripping the shovel tightly as I went inside.

A man stood in the kitchen, shouting, "Callie? Callie, are you here?" A tall, thin man. Brown hair. Unassuming, at least from the back.

Still holding the shovel, I broke my silence, "Who are you?"

The man whirled around, bright green eyes landing on me. I knew I'd seen him before; it was his eyes that gave him away. The man from the coffee shop. The one who would not stop staring at Stella. "Who the fuck are you?" he asked, not having the good sense to be frightened.

I gave him my most charming, disarming smile. It was a smile that fooled damn near everyone I met, and I wouldn't have it any other way. "I'm Killian, Stella's boss." My fingers gripped the shovel tighter, my leather glove clenching.

"I'm just here looking for my sister, since no one answers my fucking texts anymore," he said.

"Oh, you're her brother?" I played innocent, played coy. I flung a thumb over my shoulder, pointing to the door that led to the garage. This house was small; it didn't have a backdoor, thankfully. And the garage was the perfect place to end this. "She's out back. Come on. I'm sure she'll be happy to see you." I spun and started to go, and the man—who mustn't have been more than twenty-two years old—followed me begrudgingly.

When he stepped foot into the garage, he said, "What the hell are you doing here this early on a Sunday anyway? Don't tell me you're sleeping with my sister—"

I stood between him and the door that would lead to the backyard. When he spoke, I abruptly stopped walking, causing him to ram into my back and curse at me. I turned to him, watching as he shook his head and swore again.

This one…he had a mouth on him. I didn't like him.

"What the fuck?" he asked, taking a single step back when he noticed how intently I gripped the shovel. I didn't give him the chance to say more.

I moved swiftly, no hesitation, as fast as a man could possibly move. All it took was two seconds for me to lift the shovel and hit the metal against his temple, so quickly and so hard I heard the familiar crack of bone against steel reverberate through the air.

The man collapsed, his body trembling and his eyes blinking a few times before he stopped moving entirely. Nerves. Sometimes it happened. What I would really like to see is whether or not a head was still capable of blinking even after being severed. I'd heard stories of chickens running around headless.

That would be a fun thing to see, I think.

I had a long to-do list now—move his car, handle his body, deal with the corpse in the flower bed…not to mention sanitize the garage after it was said and done. But I allowed myself the time to kneel beside him and reach into his pocket. Pulling out his wallet, I saw his name was John Woods.

My eyes flicked to his bleeding form. "Well, John Woods," I paused, placing his wallet in my back pocket, near my own, "looks like you've had a bit of bad luck. Don't worry, though. I'll take good care of you." Indeed, I would. I had to, if I wanted to protect Stella.

I'd found my next angel.

Thank you for reading! Please think about leaving a review, even if it's a short one. They really make us indie authors happy (and let us know that people are actually reading our work). Twenty words and a star—that's all it takes!

Also, I love talking about books (not just mine. Any book. I LOVE books!) in general on my Twitter: www.twitter.com/CandaceWondrak and on Instagram: www.instagram.com/CandaceWondrak

My Facebook Group: Candace's Cult of Captivation where you can get all the updates on new releases!

Made in the USA
Las Vegas, NV
19 January 2023

65914441R00146